"*Little Girl in the Mirror,* a book of creative non-fiction, has the feel of a novel; is a masterful glimpse of history, and a loving memoir."
—Sheldon Currie, Author, Playwright

"A bildungsroman, this simple compassionate tale sticks with you long after reading the final words on the page. You come away affected by Cathy's story—wishing you could reach inside the pages and give the lonely girl a hug."
—David McPherson, Author of
The Legendary Horseshoe Tavern: A Complete History

"Tara Mondou weaves various threads from her family's past— faded photographs, oft-told tales, intimate revelations— into *Little Girl in the Mirror, Cathy's Story:* a poignant telling of her mother's resilience during a childhood filled with cruelty and neglect."
—Martin de Groot, Program Editor,
Promenade Community Radio Magazine,
CKWR 98.5 & Former Arts and Culture columnist
for the Waterloo Region Record

"An intricate tapestry among women is weaved and rooted in resilience and determination. Desperation, betrayal and isolation are veiled on tumultuous journeys of endurance and endless courage."
—Silvana Sangiuliano, Author, Poet

"*Little Girl in the Mirror* tells the tale of courage, disappointment, strife and love; a story that reminds us of the legacy of parenting and how one generation's experience indelibly colours the next."
—Theresa Albert, Author, Innkeeper,
Communications Consultant, Nutritionist

"Evoking a true sense of place and character through rich descriptions, Mondou invites readers deep into this moving story about taking risks, learning to forgive, and having the courage to move on."

— Jennifer Dinsmore, Freelance Editor

Little Girl in the Mirror was a book that I just couldn't put down. I was so drawn to the characters and their settings; what a flood of emotions they created!"

—Marilyn Helmer, Author of *Fog Cat*

"This book is about the complex relationships between mothers and daughters; a story about love, loneliness, yearning, neglect, and second chances. By drawing the reader back through the rich tapestry of a family's history, Mondou presents a heartwarming and sad yet beautiful tale of strong women."

—Mark Leslie (Lefebvre), Author,
Professional Speaker, Bookseller

"An incredible book and a fabulous story! One minute I was smiling, the next I was crying."

—Leslie Gordon Christie, Health & Lifestyle Specialist,
Host The Buff Mom TV

"This is a book that will haunt long after the covers are closed."

—Jockie Loomer-Kruger, Author/Illustrator
of *Valley Child - A Memoir*

Little Girl in the Mirror

Cathy's Story

TARA MONDOU

"My first experience in Ontario was the first of many disappointments and shattered expectations. Mom always talked so well of Ontario, I was anxious to see it even though I didn't want to leave Nana."

"Life at Mrs. Wrenn's was where I learned to feel I was too big, too stupid, unloved, and uncared for."

"All my memories there are terrible. I hate thinking about them. I never told my mother anything, so she tells me. Since I've grown up, I tried to figure out why there was no bond between me and Mom and why I don't think I trusted her to defend me. She seemed afraid of Mrs. Wrenn. That made me afraid too."

Taken from the diary of Catherine Barron
September, 1989

This is a work of creative nonfiction. The events and people depicted in this story are portrayed to the best of Tara Mondou's ability; inspired by a collection of letters, photographs, and memories of childhood stories. While all the stories in this book are true, they may not be entirely factual, and remain alive today only from the perspective of Catherine Barron; who is no longer with us to tell the story herself.

For Lilianne and Amelia,
May you be blessed with her strength…

For Ronnie,
Wherever we go, whatever we do, we're going to go through it together…

For Mom,
I miss you…

CONTENTS

PREFACE

My mom always told me stories about her heart-wrenching childhood. When she was a baby, her mother gave her up to her grandmother, and left her in Cape Breton, Nova Scotia, until she took her back at five years old and brought her to Stratford, Ontario. All her life my mom shared stories with me, about the evil woman they lived with and how the woman took away her ability to trust and love her mother. I think she was trying to make me understand her pain; this was a hurt she could never get over.

As a child, I didn't like these stories, I didn't want to hear about the woman who was mean to my mom, and I especially didn't want to hear about how my grandmother didn't save her. I told her she was exaggerating and that it probably wasn't that bad. I basically told her to get over it. She stopped talking about it and I thought that was for the best.

But after my mother died and I found her diary and realized just how much this woman affected her life as a child, I thought about my two little girls and couldn't imagine them going through what my mom had to go through. I felt the need to acknowledge my mother's stories, and by writing them down finally validating her, and her childhood.

Mom, I wish I had listened more, supported you more, understood you better. Through writing your story, I feel like I have taken little Cathy's hand and I have saved her, held her, and loved her.

This is your story...

Little Girl in the Mirror

in the

Cathy's Story

Rita Barron and Peggy Dunphy

RITA

The Women's Residence-Summer 1944

Rita Barron and her best friend, Peggy Dunphy, stepped off the train on a beautiful summer afternoon in early August, 1944. The train ride from Sydney, Nova Scotia to Brantford, Ontario had been a long one, but the non-stop talk of starting their new lives as "women war workers" kept the girls so excited that the trip went by in no time.

"Oh, Rita! Wait till you see how great Brantford is! There is a military base, with you couldn't guess how many soldiers!" said Peggy. "They're crawling all over the place!"

Peggy went on and on about how much fun they were going to have on their big adventure. They would be on their own, away from their parents and the nuns at school. They would be making their own money, their own decisions, and for once, would be in charge of their own lives.

Rita and Peggy had been the best of friends ever since they were little girls. They went to the same school and the same church and played together every day; their fathers even worked together in the mine down on the 1B road. The girls always had so much fun together. In the summer, they spent their time laughing and running through the fields picking blueberries and going to the shore to swim; and ice skating and stomping through the high snow drifts in the winter. They were always being silly and teasing one another. They even had nicknames for each other; Rita was "Stuff" and Peggy was "Pudge". Stuff and Pudge were both skinny as rails, and that's what they thought was so funny about their nicknames.

As teenagers they spent hours together talking about movie stars, doing their hair in the latest fashions, and looking through magazines at stylish clothes and shoes. They dreamed of leaving Cape Breton and moving to a big city like Montreal or Toronto. Rita's mother's sister, whom they called Aunt Agie, married a man named Joe Serafinis and moved to Montreal. Whenever Aunt Agie would come back home, Rita and Peggy would sit for hours asking her all about the restaurants and the people and excitement of living in a big city. It wouldn't be long before an opportunity to move away from Cape Breton would present itself to the girls.

Their adventure started in early spring when Peggy came running up Woodward Street to Rita's house waving the letter she had in her hand. She couldn't wait to tell Rita what she found out from her aunt who lived in Brantford, Ontario.

"Oh, Stuff! Wait till you hear this! My aunt wrote my mother and said that she thinks I should move to Ontario, and soon!" Peggy got comfortable on Rita's bed and told her all about the letter.

Her aunt said that companies and businesses had geared up for the war effort in the early 1940s. Factories all over Brantford were hiring women war workers from across Canada, and hundreds of girls travelled to Brantford from out East, out West, and the Prairies. Girls were working as assembly line inspectors, welders, and as lathe operators, making parts for the Avro Lancaster and the de Havilland Mosquito bomber.

Neither of the girls really knew what those were, but it sure sounded exciting!

A company called Cockshutt Plow, who just recently opened Cockshutt Moulded Aircraft, had to change over to war production as well, and needed girls to work in their factory. Brantford had become a very exciting city since the war started. It was only five years ago that King George VI and his wife, Queen Elizabeth, came to visit from England. What was even more exciting was that Gene Autry came to the city in 1942, to help raise funds for bomb victims in London. Students got the day off school and everyone in the city went downtown to see the movie star.

Because the military set up a Service Flying Training School and an Army Basic Training Camp, Brantford had become an "Armed Forces" city. They even had a group that workers could belong to called, the Community Wartime Recreation Council (C.W.R.C.), who planned fun events and activities for the workers like amateur shows, photography and drama classes, sports, and best of all, card nights!

"Oh, Peggy! I want to go with you! I want to go on an adventure and this sounds like the perfect thing!" Rita jumped up, her thoughts racing. "You have to come up to our house again tomorrow and tell Mama and Daddy what your aunt wrote. Somehow we have to convince them that I should go with you."

The girls decided that Peggy would come back once Daddy was home from work the next day.

Mama and Daddy sat at the table with their cups of tea and listened to everything Peggy had to tell them about moving to Brantford. Daddy lit a cigarette and didn't say a word while he puffed and fiddled with the half empty pack of Export "A"'s. Peggy talked about how the girls would work at Cockshutt making parts for airplanes and about living in a "girls only" dormitory. Mama and Daddy stayed silent, so Rita quickly explained that she would send money home to help with the younger ones. Daddy raised an eyebrow at that; they certainly could use more money to feed all those mouths.

Mama was worried about where Rita would live. She didn't want any daughter of hers to be living just anywhere without some sort of supervision. Peggy assured Mama that the girls would live in the Women's Staff House, which they called the "Women's Residence". Each wing of the house had its own matron to make sure the girls were taken care of, and apparently the house was on a street called Aberdeen, which made Mama feel better because Woodward Street was located in New Aberdeen, or Number 2, as most people referred to it.

Daddy stood up and walked out of the house after Peggy and Rita finished explaining the situation. Mama said that Daddy would have to think about it and that Rita shouldn't be surprised if Daddy wouldn't let her go. Frank Barron thought the world of his eldest daughter, and his wife knew his heart would break if she left him.

The weeks passed and Rita waited for her father to make his decision. Every time she tried to talk to him about moving to Ontario he would walk out of the house, or light a cigarette and go silent. She knew how much he loved her, and she loved him, but she couldn't stay in Cape Breton forever, and nothing was more important to her than starting a new life up in Ontario.

She loved Mama with all her heart, but she didn't want to turn out like her or have her life. She wasn't going to marry a miner or a fisherman and live in a shack or a company house and worry about trying to make ends meet her whole life. She wasn't going to take the bus back and forth to work in Glace Bay every day or up to Dominion to play bingo on Friday nights. As much as she loved the seashore and the ocean, the blue skies and the cliffs, she knew she wasn't going to stay in Cape Breton.

Although she wanted to leave the Island, she didn't exactly hate her life at home. Sometimes it was hard when Daddy didn't pull up enough coal to buy food and clothes for all the kids, but Mama and Daddy did their best and Rita seldom felt that they went without. In a way, Daddy kind of spoiled Rita; he hardly ever made her do her chores and Mama only made her do the dishes and the laundry once in a while because they knew that Rita was busy keeping up her grades.

Ever since she was a little girl, Rita felt loved by her family and by the nuns at school. She always liked going to school, she was very smart and had an easy time learning. Her family thought she was cute as a button, and as long as she could remember, friends and family were always asking her to sing them a song. She knew every word to the old Irish ballads and hymns her aunts in Ingonish had taught her.

As a teenager, Rita was one of the most attractive girls in high school. She had long black hair, pretty brown eyes, a beautiful smile, and a slim figure. She was always asked to the dance and there was often a boy or two walking her home, carrying her books, and asking her to sing or tell them a joke.

All her brothers and sisters loved her too, and would do anything for her. The girls would ask her to comb their hair or help them with their homework, and the boys loved to hear her stories about funny things that happened at school. Rita was happy to be with her nine younger brothers and sisters, but after a while she would get antsy and go out the door and up the road looking to see what her friends were up to.

Besides Peggy, she often hung around with her girlfriend from across the street, Lolly O'Neill. Daddy didn't like this friendship much because he couldn't stand Lolly's father, Leo. But whenever Rita could sneak off with Lolly, they would walk the tracks to nearby Glace Bay and have fun looking at the boats in the harbour or walking along Glace Bay Beach and eating chips from the old wagon on Commercial Street.

When Rita was out, her sisters, Kay and Alice, would help their mother with the younger ones. Kay never seemed to mind because she loved to cook and clean and get everyone organized. But Alice, on the other hand, couldn't understand why her mother just let Rita go roaming around wherever and whenever she wanted. Alice could often be overheard complaining that there was too much work to do around the house—dishes and laundry and diapers and cooking; it never ended—and that she was always left doing Rita's chores. Even the younger sisters, Molly and Tussie, were put to work as soon as they were old enough.

Nothing made Alice madder than when sometimes, early in the morning, when it was still dark, Daddy would wake all the kids up to go in the fields to pick moss.

Rita would just moan and roll over and say she was too tired to pick, and he would let her go back to sleep while the rest of them shuffled tiredly out the door and into the dark to pick moss before the sun came up. Alice didn't understand how Rita got away with it. She didn't think Rita was that special; she wasn't the only one who was smart and pretty. Daddy was always telling Alice that she would make a good wife one day and that she was a hard worker and a good Catholic. So why was it that he let Rita get away with murder while the rest of them had to make up for it?

After Rita finished high school and started working in Glace Bay, she started feeling that there was more to life than what Mama and Daddy and the coal mine had to offer. So when Peggy came running up the road that day and told her all about life in Ontario, she knew she was leaving.

In her family, there were ones who would stay, and ones who would go—and Rita was going. She imagined that her sister Kay, who she always called Katie, and her brother Doug, would go too, but the rest of them—Alice and the younger ones—they would stay. They would stay on Cape Breton Island, go to church, work hard, and try their best to be happy. But Rita wanted more than to just be happy. She wanted excitement and adventure, and she couldn't wait any longer. Peggy was already making her plans to go and if Rita didn't get permission from her parents soon, Peggy would leave without her—and Rita couldn't imagine her life in Cape Breton without her.

One night after supper, after all the dishes were washed and dried and the little ones were in bed, Mama sat rocking in her chair by the stove, saying her evening prayers. Rita was sitting on the sofa trying to read a book, but found she was preoccupied looking out the window and daydreaming about leaving Cape Breton. She heard Mama clear her throat.

"Rita."

Rita looked over at her mother with concern because her voice sounded strained. Mama put her prayers down and said, "Daddy has decided that you can go up to Ontario." She sounded as if she were fighting back tears.

"Oh Mama! He did?" Rita couldn't believe her ears. She jumped up from the couch and ran to her mother. She dropped down to her knees and took Mama's hand.

"Oh thank you, thank you, thank you! You won't regret this Mama, you'll see. I'll send money home to you every month and I'll come back down home to visit all the time."

Rita's mother looked down at her eldest daughter with sad eyes. She didn't want Rita to leave. She loved her so much and was worried about what life would be like without her beautiful, smart girl. She gave Rita a small smile, squeezed her hand and said that even though Rita would be allowed to go to Ontario with Peggy, she would have to wait until she turned 20 years old before she could go.

So, on June 14, Rita announced that she had bought her train ticket and was leaving the first week of August. Her birthday was really on June 13, but on the year she was born, the 13th happened to be on a Friday, and there was no way Mama was going to have her first child be born on such a wicked day, so she just let on to everyone that her little baby girl was born on the 14th. Rita thought Mama was too superstitious, but the way she looked at it, she got to celebrate her birthday twice! She had so many friends and so much to celebrate that she needed two days to get through it all anyway.

Even though Mama and Daddy said she could go to Ontario, she was still shocked that they actually let her get on the train that day. Daddy hugged her tight, pressed some money into her hand, and before she noticed his eyes filling up with tears, he walked away, fishing the cigarette pack out of his shirt pocket. Rita put her arms around her mother and hugged her, and for a minute it seemed like Mama wasn't going to let her go, but Rita gently pulled away and took a few steps back. She didn't want Mama to be sad, but she had to go, she just had to start her new adventure.

When Rita and Peggy arrived at the Women's Residence, Rita was in awe. Four hundred women lived in the dormitory. Most of them had left home for the first time, and for most of them, this was their first real job. Imagine, working in a factory—just like a man!

The House Mother brought them to their room and after showing them which bed was which, starting rhyming off all the rules. There was a strict curfew and all girls had to be in the house by 10 o'clock. They were allowed to have visitors, but the callers would have to meet the girls in the Dating Parlour, and they couldn't stay out after half past eight. No men were allowed in the rest of the house, not the hallways, not the kitchen and especially not in the dorm rooms. The girls were excited to find out that they had their own beauty parlour where they could get their hair done and their nails painted. All the girls wanted bright red nail polish on their finger nails and their toe nails.

They wore their hair in pageboys—some in the short style and a few in the long style like Rita Hayworth and Loretta Young. There was even a games room where the girls could play ping pong and other activities, but best of all, they had their very own bowling alley!

"Well, Stuff, we finally made it!" Peggy said with a wide smile as she put her suitcase on her bed.

"Oh, Pudge! Can you imagine? We'll be working and going out and singing and dancing. What a hoot it's going to be!" Rita said as she rushed across the room to her friend and hugged her with all her might.

Peggy hugged her back and laughed, "We're going to have a hell of a good time!"

Rita and Cathy

CHAPTER ONE

Stratford-Spring 1961

"You know you're my best friend, right?" The dark haired, dark-eyed, 10-year-old girl asked as she peered at her reflection in the mirror. It was late afternoon and the dust motes were dancing in the sunlight that was streaming through the open window across the room. It was getting hot in the apartment and the ceiling fan only worked when it was on low. Cathy was leaning across her mother's dusty old dresser where the room's only mirror leaned against the cracked plaster wall. As she gazed at herself, Cathy wasn't sure about what she saw today. She couldn't help but notice the uneven black bangs that her mom cut with those dull scissors the other day.

"I hate those bangs," she said out loud.

Why couldn't she have long, beautiful hair like the girls at school? The girls at school were all so pretty and had such nice clothes. She really only had the two thin dresses that Nana bought her at the end of her summer vacation and the one light blue cardigan she wore almost every day, no matter how hot it was. She pulled up her cardigan sleeve and looked at the mole on her right forearm.

"Yuck. I hate it; it's so ugly," she said to the empty room.

She rubbed at the mole, hoping somehow it would just go away. She sighed and pulled the sleeve back down. She noticed that the sleeve didn't quite make it all the way to her wrist.

She looked at the girl in the mirror for a few more minutes. She often wondered what the girl was thinking. How she was feeling. Sometimes, on days like this when she didn't go to school, she would stare in the mirror for hours trying to figure the girl out. She would look deep into her friend's eyes to see if she felt sad or happy, excited, or scared. Sometimes she thought the girl felt lonely or worried. Maybe the girl just missed Nana, Janey, and Marlene, who still lived together back on Cape Breton Island.

Even after all these years Cathy still wished that her mother had just left her at Nana's, where she felt safe and loved, and surrounded by family who cared about her. She often wondered why she had to leave Cape Breton to come and live in Ontario.

From as far back as she could remember, she lived with Nana and Papa in Glace Bay, Cape Breton. Nana said she was only 18 months old when her mother, Rita, gave her to Nana to take care of. Janey and Marlene, who were both a few years younger than Cathy, lived there too. The three of them were like sisters, although Cathy never knew where they came from. Nana seemed to be too old to be Janey's mother and it didn't seem like Marlene had any parents at all. The rumour was that Papa brought Marlene home from a poker game one night. It seemed kind of crazy, but that was the story.

Back then, her mom lived most of the time in Brantford, Ontario, working and trying to find a nice place for the two of them to live. She would come "down home" in the summertime, and Cathy was always so excited to spend a few short weeks with her mom picking blueberries in the fields and running up and down the shore. When her mom would leave to go back up to Ontario, Cathy would settle into the life she had with Nana and Papa.

Cathy and Marlene walked to school every day, but "that little sook" Janey got to stay home with Nana most of the time. She was small for her age and sick a lot of the time, so Nana always felt "sorry for her."

Even though they went to school together, Marlene didn't usually go to class. She often wandered off somewhere, doing God only knew what. Marlene never really liked school.

The three girls all slept in the same bed, and in the freezing cold of winter Nana would put heavy coats on them for warmth. In the mornings they got dressed behind the wood stove because the house was so cold. There was no plumbing in the house, so they had to use the creepy old outhouse out in the yard. Cathy was too scared to go to the outhouse at night, so Nana kept a little pot for her to go in when she needed it.

The three girls always looked forward to the spring. Papa kept chickens and a mean old rooster in the yard, and when spring finally came around the girls would spend most of their time outside feeding the chickens and running for their lives away from the crazy rooster. Before Cathy knew it, summer would roll around again and her mom would step off the train looking beautiful with her stylish outfits, her red lipstick, and her long hair done in the popular pageboy style.

It never occurred to Cathy to wonder why she had lived in Nova Scotia all those years and not with her mom up in Ontario. It was just always how it was. She had lived at Nana and Papa's at 9 Woodward Street in a small house with reddish-brown tarpaper shingles. She always thought it was made out of brick, but when she touched it one time she saw that it was just paper stuff. It was built on raised ground on land that was wild and windy. It was all long grass, wild flowers, and bushes and scrub. In the back of the house was the chicken coop with a dirt yard, and small sheds and shacks that were falling apart all over the field.

Cathy knew that there used to be a front porch on the house, and if someone were to sit there, they would have a view of the road and of the O'Neills, who lived across the way. Papa and Leo O'Neill had a big fight one time, and Papa yelled that the last thing he wanted, was to walk out the front door and see that damn O'Neill staring at him from across the road.

So, he took a sledge hammer from one of the sheds and started smashing the porch to bits. Wood and nails went flying everywhere, and Cathy's aunts, uncles, and her cousins, ran to hide. After the porch was demolished, Papa gathered up all of the wood and started boarding up the front door. The wood was all crisscrossed and messy looking.

Nana just stood in the yard in her house dress shaking her head back and forth as if she were wondering how the family was going to get in and out of the house from now on. They never had a front door again.

Cathy had many aunts and uncles. They didn't all live at the house in the early 1950s, most of them had moved out after they got married and had their own kids. Rita, Doug, Kay, and Mickey were all up in Ontario. Alice and her husband, Johnny Ryan, lived down the road, and Molly and her husband, Rolfe, lived up in Dominion on Mitchell Avenue. Tussie lived with her husband, Jimmy McGillivray, down in the Row, and Francis, Joanie, and Rose all lived in the house with Nana and Papa.

When Papa came home from work and was in the kind of mood he was in during the porch incident, any kids, grandkids, and even the neighbour kids that were home, took off to get out of his way. But it was hard to blame Papa for his temper.

Frank Barron worked in the pit since his 20s, and no matter how much coal he brought up, there was never much money left on the pay after the store was paid off. Instead of coming home and giving what was left over to Nana, so she could buy flour to make bread, he oftentimes finished his shift at the mine and stopped for a few drinks before he headed up the train tracks and crossed the field to their house. His plan never was to work in the mines or to even live in Glace Bay for that matter.

The Barrons were from Ingonish; from wide open spaces, breathtaking landscapes, the ocean, the cliffs, and Cape Smokey in the Appalachian Mountains. His father's family originally came from Ireland, they farmed and fished and lived off the land.

His mother's family, the Brewers and Doucettes, were from the reserve; the women were Mi'kmaq Indians. His grandmother, Susan Brewer Doucette, was a wise woman, an herbalist, and a storyteller. She was well-known and highly respected; she had lived to be 104 years of age.

The story was told that the Barron boys came down to Glace Bay in the early 1920s, looking for work. They needed money to buy farm tools and materials, and had told their family they would only work in the pits for a short time to get the money together. While they worked, they stayed in a boarding house run by a widow and her daughters.

The widow's name was Mary Anne McIsaac Hanrahan. Mary Anne was a strong, independent woman who, although having lost her husband when her children were small, went on to raise all ten of them by herself and did pretty well on her own.

One of Mary Anne's daughter's names was Catherine. Frank and Catherine fell in love quickly, but once Frank made his money, he wanted Catherine to go back with him to Ingonish. She told him that she would not leave her mother, so on November 29, 1923, Francis James Barron married Catherine

Jane Hanrahan. Shortly after, in June 1924, Catherine gave birth to Rita Marie Barron, and they lived and worked in Colliery Number Two, just up from the 1B road.

Cathy loved hearing the stories of how Papa and Nana met and got married and about how they had ten children of their own; worked hard, went to church and did their best to live life on the wind-swept cliffs of Cape Breton. Cathy had been so happy living with her grandparents and her cousins, and although it was only for the first five years of her young life, they were the happiest memories she had.

Left to right: Rita, Marlene, Janey, Cathy

Front: Bimbo

CHAPTER TWO

Stratford-Spring 1961

Thinking about her life in Cape Breton made Cathy feel so lonesome. She saw that the little girl in the mirror's eyes started to well up with tears and her chin started to quiver. Cathy saw her friend was about to cry, so she squeezed her lips together and closed her eyes tight. When she opened them again, the little girl's eyes were wide, but dry, and her chin was still.

She sighed and pushed herself away from the dresser and went back to the kitchen to put the kettle on. Once the tea was ready, she picked up the latest book she was reading and curled up on the old, worn couch. She had at least a couple of hours before her mom got home from working in the Laundry at the Stratford General Hospital. Hopefully her mom wouldn't find out that she didn't go to school again today.

She sipped her tea and got comfortable and opened the book to where she left off. The story was just getting good when she heard a noise in the hall.

Just someone walking down the hall to the bathroom, she thought to herself as she quickly glanced at the door to make sure she'd locked it after her mom left for work that morning.

She and her mom lived in a second floor apartment above a stationery store at 50 Wellington Street in Stratford. They'd only been there for a few months since they moved from Mrs. Wrenn's house. The apartment was really just one big room with high ceilings and a single window. There was a small kitchen with a hotplate and one cupboard for their dishes. In the corner by the apartment's window was the bird cage. Cathy's mom loved birds. This one's name was Mickey and it made a lot of noise and a lot of mess, but he was good company and it was fun when Cathy's mom would take him out of his cage and let him sit on the footstool. On the other side of the room was a tiny bedroom with a saggy double bed they had to share. There was the old dresser with the mirror, and the dusty couch with a chair that didn't match. Cathy thought the curtains were ugly, and the walls looked like they hadn't been washed in years.

She wished her mom would clean the small apartment like Aunt Kay would have. Aunt Kay was so clean and her place in Brantford was always sparkling and smelling like bleach.

Maybe we could go and visit Aunt Kay next week, she thought to herself.

As she was thinking about Aunt Kay, one of her mom's younger sisters, she also thought about Kay's husband, Frank Larion. She was a little scared of Uncle Frank because he was kind of grumpy and wasn't very nice to Aunt Kay and her cousins. She remembered the time when she was helping Aunt Kay wax the floors, and by the time they were done, the floor was gleaming. Aunt Kay sat at the kitchen table and opened a beer to celebrate all the hard work they'd done. When Uncle Frank walked in after work, he walked right across the floor with his dirty boots! Aunt Kay didn't say a word. She just shrugged her shoulders, looked out the window, and opened another beer.

Even though Uncle Frank was sometimes mean like that, Cathy often caught him looking at her in a strange sort of way. He always looked like he was going to say something, but instead he would just smile at her sadly and look away.

As she remembered her last visit to Brantford, she heard the noise in the hall again. It sounded like someone stopped outside their door. She put the book down and looked at the crack underneath the door and saw two shadows—as if someone were standing there.

Is it a man?

She held her breath and looked at the deadbolt on the door. Whew! It's locked. Is someone going to knock?

Her mom always said she should never answer the door when she was alone.

Then she saw the doorknob move from side to side! After a moment, she heard another noise further up on the door. She looked up above the door and noticed the transom was open! She couldn't move; she was frozen to the couch. All of a sudden, she saw a hand fumbling with the transom window. She jumped off the couch and ran over to the kitchen. She saw the heavy pan her mom left drying on the counter after breakfast this morning. She looked back at the transom and saw a man's whole arm reaching into the room trying to open the window wider! She turned back to the counter and grabbed the handle of the pan and ran over to the door.

"Get away from our DOOR!!" she screamed. "I'll smash you in the head with this PAN!"

Suddenly, the man pulled his arm out of the transom. Something was moved away from the door and the shadowy feet moved away too. She heard shuffling down the hallway. Who was that? Was someone trying to get her?

Her heart was pounding; she felt like she was going to have a heart attack. She backed towards the kitchen, keeping her eyes on the door, and put the pan back on the counter. She tiptoed into the bedroom and over to the dresser and looked in the mirror.

"Do you believe what just happened to us?" she asked the reflection.

The girl's dark blue eyes were as big as saucers, and she looked really scared. Cathy reached out with her fingers and touched the reflection's cheek.

"Don't worry… Mom will be home soon. Maybe we should have gone to school today. I promise, we'll go tomorrow, OK?"

The girl in the mirror relaxed, and Cathy quietly said, "Thank God you were here with me. You really are my best friend."

She smiled her kindest smile at her friend, hoping to make her feel better. The little girl smiled back. Cathy turned away from the mirror on the dresser and tiptoed back over to the couch. She picked up her cold teacup and her book. She checked to make sure no one was looking in at her from the transom and then waited quietly for her mom to come home from the Laundry.

Rita (on the right) in the Laundry

CHAPTER THREE

Stratford-Spring 1961

"Rita! Where are you?" called the woman over the sound of the giant steam press.

It was only early April and it was already too hot in the Laundry. There was steam rising to the ceiling and hot water dripping everywhere. All the ladies had sweat running down their faces and were constantly wiping themselves down with their handkerchiefs. Even Lux and Eddy, over by the vat, were sweating bullets and had huge stains under their arms.

There were a few windows but they were placed up so high that they were of no use. There was no air coming in and no way of cooling down the heavy heat of the room.

Rita was hoping that Mrs. Jutzi wouldn't find her squatting down in her hiding spot behind the press with her back against the wall and her head in her hands. God, she just needed a few minutes to rest. What she really needed was a cigarette. Her head was killing her from the night before and all she wanted to do was get out of this laundry room and go home and go to bed. She checked her watch; two more hours. Rita pulled herself up from her spot in the corner, straightened her uniform and tucked a sweaty curl of thick black hair back under her hair net.

"I'm here, Mrs. Jutzi!" she yelled through the mist as she walked past her floor lady and back to her place at the folding table. Mrs. Jutzi shook her head as Rita went by.

"You OK, Hun?" Ella gave Rita a little smile as she returned to the table.

"Yes, Ella. Thanks. Just tired and hot, and my feet are killing me," she replied. Her right foot that she broke climbing out of the Women's Residence in Brantford still pained; she didn't think it ever healed right. Ella nudged her gently with her elbow.

"Well Honey, your face is as white as a sheet!" They both laughed tiredly at the old joke.

They had been working together since 1956 and had become fast friends. Ella Jackson was the only black friend that Rita had, and no matter what others said about their friendship, Rita always relied on Ella's soft heart and soft shoulder to lean on when she needed it. And lately, it seemed that Rita always needed to lean on someone's shoulder.

A few hours and hundreds of folded sheets later, the quitting bell finally rang. With a tired goodbye to Ella, Rita untied her apron, pulled off her hair net, and dragged herself to her locker at the end of the room. She opened it and looked at the picture of Cathy that she had taped to the inside of the door.

"My Cathy-o…," she murmured to herself. She stroked the chubby cheeks of her favourite picture of her daughter from when she was only five years old. This was the one where they sat and had a professional portrait done. The one with the two of them was at home in a frame on the wall, but Rita wanted to keep this one of Cathy with her at work. She lovingly touched the photo again, reached for her purse and her sweater, and headed straight for the employee entrance of the hospital.

Just as she was about to head out the door, her other girlfriend from the Laundry, Elinor, caught up with her.

"Where ya headed, Rita?" Elinor asked as she quickened her step to catch up.

"I'm headed home, Elinor," Rita said as she made her way down the sidewalk. "I have to get off my feet. I need to have a hot cup of tea and some toast, and I want to see how my Cathy's doing. Plus, I think the maintenance man is supposed to fix our transom this afternoon, so I want to be there when he comes."

Elinor opened her mouth to say something, but Rita quickly cut her off.

"You know I don't like leaving her home alone after school Elinor, and she's already been home for hours, she's probably starving," she said as she stopped and turned to her friend.

Elinor nodded and smiled to herself and opened her purse to take out her cigarette pack. She fished one out, stopped for a moment to light it, took a long drag, and exhaled—all the while with that knowing grin on her face. Rita really liked Elinor because she was always good for a laugh and liked to play cards on Friday nights, but Rita knew what was coming next and she got ready to stick to her plan. Rita had promised Cathy that she would come home right after work. They were going to talk about Cathy's birthday party that was coming up on the 18th. Rita couldn't believe she was going to be 11 years old already! Where did the time go? It seemed like only yesterday when she found out she was pregnant.

It was April, 1950 and she was as big as a house; nothing fit her, she couldn't get her shoes on, and she couldn't go anywhere. Rita was still boarding with Ma Edwards in the house at 81 Allenby Avenue in Brantford. She had been living there since they closed the Women's Residence in 1945. Ma Edwards was a kind woman, and Rita loved living with her. And since Ma's son and his wife got married and moved out, Rita and Ma had the whole house to themselves.

Until recently, Rita had a job babysitting a cute little girl named Lally, but she had to quit her job because she was getting too big to take care of little Lally properly. Ma was giving her some time to have the baby, rest for a while, and then look for work again so she could pay the rent.

Rita's sister, Kay, came by every day after work to help her get ready for the baby. Together they made sure that Rita had sleepers, baby blankets, and a few bottles. They had the little bassinet all ready, and on the change table there was a stack of cloth diapers, a jar of Penaten cream, and those great big pins to hold the diaper together.

Kay finished washing the last of the baby clothes, folded them neatly, and put them in the drawer. She looked around to see what else she could do. She had already cleaned the floors, done the dishes, and made the bed. God love Rita, but she wasn't much of a homemaker, and Ma Edwards was getting too old to keep house.

Rita was lying on the couch with her feet propped up on a pillow. Kay could hardly see her head because her tummy was so big. She went over to Rita and sat beside her.

"What are you gonna do, Reet? Have you decided yet?" Kay had an odd way of pushing her lower jaw out when she asked a question, and she did this now.

"I told you, Katie. I am not giving my baby up. I don't care what they say!" Rita said as she struggled to sit up.

Kay stood and pulled Rita up by the arm and then went to the kitchen to put the kettle on. Rita went in after her, sat at the table, and covered her eyes with her hands. She didn't let on to Kay, but she was terrified: terrified to give birth, to be a mom, and to do it all on her own.

For the last several months, every time she went to the hospital for a check-up, the nuns told her that she shouldn't keep the baby.

How could they think that she wouldn't keep it? She didn't know what to say or what to do; she became afraid that they had the power to take her baby away. Sometimes they would even follow her out of the hospital and down the street to the bus stop.

"You are a single woman," they'd say. "You have no home of your own and no real job. How do you expect to take care of a baby?" That was all true, but what hurt the most was when they'd say, "The father doesn't even want to marry you." And they were right. Reg Larion didn't want to marry her.

They had been dating on and off for the past couple years and Rita thought Reg was falling in love with her. He was Frank's brother and both Frank and Kay thought Rita and Reg would make a cute couple. They'd had so much fun together taking day trips to Turkey Point to go boating on Lake Erie and relaxing on the beach. Rita thought Reg was very handsome. He was a big muscular man with tanned skin and white teeth. Rita loved how he kept his hair long on top. How sometimes he'd slick it straight back or sometimes he'd let his brown curls tumble over his forehead. Reg was a quiet man, but everyone knew that if you disrespected him or his family in any way, there would be hell to pay.

Her face crumpled with the memory of their last time together when she told him she was pregnant. Reg said he couldn't marry her. He made it very clear. He couldn't marry her he said because he was in love with someone else. How can you be in love with someone else when your girlfriend is pregnant?

She shook her head. She couldn't think about him now; she would drive herself around the bend if she thought of him one more minute.

"Is that kettle boiled yet, Katie? I'm dying of thirst," she said as she pulled herself up to go and open the window. "I can't breathe in here. I need air." She struggled to pull the heavy window up.

"Here, let me get it." Kay pulled the wooden window frame up with one hand. "Go sit down and drink your tea. You're just getting yourself all excited." Kay took Rita by the shoulders and gently pushed her back into the chair. "It's not good for the baby."

Kay sat down at the table, took her hot teacup in her hands, and looked Rita in the eye. Her jaw was working its way in and out.

"What are you going to do, Rita?" she asked again.

Her question was answered on Tuesday April 18, 1950. Rita went into labour and was taken to Hamilton General Hospital. She gave birth to a healthy baby girl and named her Catherine Rita, after her mother and herself. The nuns kept coming in the nursery and insisting that Rita give the baby up.

"Let the child go to someone who can take care of her; a family with a mother and father. To people who have a nice house and can give her all the things you can't."

Rita was a good Catholic; she didn't pray as much as her Mama did, but months ago when the nuns started telling her that she'd have to give up her baby, she started to pray every day. She prayed to the Virgin Mary for guidance and to God for the strength she needed to get through this.

While she was feeding Cathy, the nun who kept at her the most came in and said, "You MUST give up that baby. God does NOT want you to keep it."

That was it. The nun couldn't use her God against her. God would never want her to give her baby away. She stood up, and with a strong clear voice she said, "I will keep this baby. She is MY baby and I will NOT give her up!" The nun was startled that this young woman, who was supposedly a good Catholic, would have the nerve to speak to her this way. She backed out of the room.

The nuns kept at her every day. They even had the priest come in, but Rita would not budge. After a while she pretended they weren't even there. She just sat in the nursery, praying for strength, and holding her baby girl. She was the sweetest little thing she ever saw, and she swore she would never let her go. After a week, the doctors finally gave Rita her papers and released her and Cathy from the hospital.

Frank and Kay drove Rita and little Cathy back to Ma Edwards' place. Ma smiled from ear to ear when she met the new baby. "My God, Rita! She looks just like you!"

After Rita gently rocked Cathy to sleep and settled her into the bassinet, she unpacked her overnight bag. At the bottom of the bag, in the envelope with all the paperwork, she found the birth certificate. It said, "Baby's name - Catherine Rita Barron, Mother - Rita Marie Barron, Father… none."

And now, her little baby was turning 11 years old. Rita was

so proud of herself for standing her ground and keeping her baby. No matter what they did, and no matter what they said, she kept her baby. She told Cathy the story every year on April 18th, of how the nuns tried to take her away, but she wouldn't let them.

Cathy would listen to the story and her eyes would get real big and she didn't say much, but Rita knew it made Cathy happy. She knew Cathy was glad that she kept her, and Rita smiled to herself knowing that no one could take that away from her. It was her proudest moment. And even though 18 months later Rita had to make the very difficult decision to ask her parents to take care of little Cathy for a few short years while she got back on her feet, found a job and a place for them to live, she knew she was making the best decision she could for her daughter.

"C'mon Rita, I know you're dying for a smoke and you must be as parched as I am after working in that hellhole all day. Let's swing by the hotel for a quick drink and then I swear we'll head home."

"No thank you, Elinor. Like I said, I have to check on my Cathy." But even as Rita said this, she could imagine a cold beer in the coolness of the Dominion Hotel uptown. She really needed a cigarette and hated smoking on the street, and the hotel was only a little bit out of the way. God, she was thirsty and the sweat was only just starting to cool down her back.

"OK, but just one Elinor, alright?" she relented.

"Sounds good to me, Kid!" Elinor laughed as they headed up the road.

Back from left to right: Joanie, Little Molly, Big Molly and Doug
Front: Janey, Papa and Marlene

CHAPTER FOUR

Cape Breton/Ontario-Early August 1955

The skies were grey and it had started raining on that sad August morning when Rita and Cathy arrived at the train station in Sydney. Cathy's mom had recently moved from Brantford to Stratford and decided that she was now ready to have Cathy live with her in Ontario. For the life of her, little five-year-old Cathy just couldn't get over having to say good bye to Nana earlier that morning.

"Leave her with me, Rita. Don't take her to Ontario," Nana said as she pulled Cathy into her big, soft arms. Cathy could feel her grandmother's body shaking and her shoulders heaving up and down.

Rita gently pulled Cathy away from her mother's embrace and put her hand on her daughter's shoulder.

"Mama, we've already talked about this. I have to take Cathy with me, she's registered to start school in the fall," she explained. "I finally have a good job and a place to live, and I want to be a good mother to Cathy. I feel sick that I left her with you and Daddy all these years, but I'm ready to have her with me now."

After a few more teary goodbyes, Rita hugged her mother, promised to write her as soon as they arrived in Ontario, and went out the door and down the road. Holding Cathy's hand, they started the long walk that took them to the Glace Bay bus station, and from there to the train station in Sydney.

Cathy spent the whole bus ride trying to hide the tears that were streaming down her cheeks. She could still feel Nana's big arms around her and Nana's body heaving with silent sobs and all Cathy wanted to do was cry her eyes out, but she kept quiet because she didn't want her mother to be upset with her. Although Cathy's heart was broken after leaving Nana, by the time the bus dropped them off at the train station, she started to wonder about the idea of spending so much time with her beautiful mother on the long train ride to Brantford, Ontario.

They had arrived with plenty of time to wait for the first train of the day to pull into the station and Cathy noticed that her mother was dressed in the cotton dress with the pretty flowers that she wore when she was traveling. To go with her dress, she had her white purse and her matching white pumps. She had her black hair styled in a shorter version of her famous pageboy and was wearing her usual red lipstick.

Little Cathy had her best blue dress on with her white sandals and the tiny purse that Nana gave her earlier that morning. Inside the purse, along with a few coins she had saved from the pay, Nana had given Cathy her favourite white mint candies that she always kept hidden in her house dress pocket. But the best part was that Nana had given Cathy her very own compact mirror!

Nana always had a compact in her purse, and when she would finally get a moment to sit down and rest her feet, she would fish her compact out of her old black purse, open it up, and slowly say, "Oh my Lord! What a sight!"

Her big brown eyes would open real wide and she would shake her head from side to side as if she couldn't believe that it was her reflection in the little mirror. She would smooth down her grey hair, put her palm against her cheek, and say, "What a pretty girl." Then she would roll her eyes up to the heavens, say a silent prayer, and then roll her eyes in your direction to see if you caught on to her little joke. She would never laugh or let on that she was being silly.

Cathy always felt so comfortable with Nana, but she often felt a little shy around Rita. After all, she hadn't really been alone with her since she could remember. Whenever Rita visited Cape Breton, there was always a kitchen full of family and neighbours all gathered round waiting for their chance to visit with her.

Even when they went down to the shore, all of Rita's sisters would run to catch up with her as she ran through the fields to get to the path that led down to the ocean. The place to swim was called the "Cubby" by everyone who lived there. Sometimes they would bring a blanket and a picnic basket with a few things to eat from Nana's larder.

During those times, Cathy never took her eyes off the woman she knew was her mother. Sometimes Rita would notice Cathy looking at her, and she'd run over and swoop her up and turn her around in the air, laughing the whole time. Although Cathy liked being in Rita's arms, she was a little nervous that she would drop her, so she was always happy when her feet hit the ground again and she could run over to Nana or her Aunt Molly to find safety in their arms.

While they waited for the train, Cathy opened up the compact and looked in the mirror. Looking back at her was a little girl, five years old, with big dark blue eyes and chubby cheeks. She loved the girl in the mirror and although most of the time the girl looked happy, when Cathy looked really closely, she could tell that the little girl sometimes looked worried or scared.

She wondered how she felt today; about leaving Cape Breton and taking a train all the way up to Ontario. She looked deep into the little girl's eyes and saw that she looked unsure and a little nervous. She smiled her best smile at the little girl and hoped it would make her feel better. She sighed with relief when she saw the little girl smile back at her. Cathy closed the compact and put it back in her purse.

She took two mints out of the Kleenex they were wrapped in, and shyly offered one to her mother. Rita smiled, popped it into her mouth and turned to look down the track at the approaching train. As the train pulled noisily into the station a sense of excitement overwhelmed Cathy, and when she looked up at her mother, Rita turned back towards her, smiled again, and squeezed her hand.

"Alright, Cathy-o, it's time to start our new adventure!" She picked up their blue suitcases and they climbed the stairs onto the train.

Once they found their seats and got their tickets stamped, Rita took Cathy to the dining car. They bought one sandwich and a small pot of tea and then sat at a window seat where they shared their little lunch. Rita said she had to be careful with the money she saved for the train ride back to Ontario, so they would share one sandwich and hopefully that would tide them over until later in the evening.

Cathy had never been on a train before, and although she was starving, she couldn't help but climb up on her knees and stare out the window where she could see the fields and trees go by. Soon they were crossing over the Canso Causeway and heading towards Truro where they would have to switch trains. Everything was going by so fast, she started to feel dizzy, so she sat back, took a sip of tea, and started eating her half of the sandwich. While she chewed her small bite, she looked at her mother. Rita had finished her lunch, lit a cigarette, and was staring out the window.

It seemed to Cathy that her mother wasn't really looking at the scenery; she had a far off look in her eyes as if she were somewhere else. Suddenly she blinked, turned her head, and looked at Cathy, almost as if she were surprised to see her there. Then she smiled and said, "Oh, Cathy, I'm so happy you're coming up to Ontario with me. We're going to have so much fun together, you and I." She reached over and swept Cathy's long bangs out of her eyes.

She was so beautiful and her smile was so sweet that Cathy's heart filled with a warm feeling, and all she wanted to do was go to her mother, curl up on her lap, and stay in her arms forever. Just as Cathy was about to go to her, Rita turned back to the window, took another long puff from her cigarette, and got that faraway look in her eyes again.

Cathy sank back down into her seat, picked up the last bit of her sandwich, and while turning to the window, took another bite and continued to watch her world go by. She felt a lump form in her throat and although she was looking forward to the adventure with her mother, she wondered if she would see Cape Breton and the shore, Nana and Papa, Janey and Marlene, the chickens, and everything else she loved, ever again.

From the back, left to right: Frank Larion and Doug, Rose Marie, Elsie and
Walter, Cathy and Rita

CHAPTER FIVE

Brantford-Early August 1955

They arrived at the Brantford train station, and after two days of being cooped up in the stuffy train they were glad to get outside and breathe in the fresh air. Cathy noticed that something was missing, and then she realized it was the salt air and the distant cry of seagulls that she was used to down home.

"Reet! Cathy! You're finally here!" Rita's little sister Kay came running across the platform. She was a tiny, dark-haired woman with a smile that beamed and eyes that twinkled. She was slight, but was able to get them both in her strong arms and give them a big hug. She stepped back, bent over, and put her hands on Cathy's shoulders.

"Oh, Cathy! My God! I haven't seen you since you were 18 months old. I can't believe that you're not a baby anymore." She knelt down right on the platform and pulled Cathy to her. She hugged her so tight, Cathy almost couldn't breathe.

"C'mon girlie, put your arms around your Aunt Katie and give me a hug."

Cathy slowly put her arms around her aunt's shoulders. Aunt Kay gently pressed Cathy's head into the warm space between her neck and shoulder and rocked her back and forth. Cathy took a deep breath and let out a long sigh and let her Aunt Kay hold her. She suddenly felt like crying because this hug reminded her so much of Nana. From that moment on, she loved Aunt Kay from a deep place in her heart and she would continue to love her for the rest of her life.

When Aunt Kay finally pulled away and looked at her little niece, she smiled and wiped away her tears, just as they started to fall. "I'm so happy to have you here, Cathy."

Kay stood up, took Cathy's suitcase and her hand, and looked at her older sister.

"Hiya, Reet! How was the trip? How's Mama?"

As the little girl and the two sisters walked off the platform and over to the parking lot, they quickly got caught up on how things were down home, how Mama and Daddy were working hard, and how the rest of the family were doing.

"Here they are, Frank!" Kay called out to a handsome man standing beside a big black car parked in the shade of a tree.

"Hello, Rita," he said as he leaned in and gave her an awkward peck on the cheek.

"Hello, Frank," Rita said as she quickly looked away from him. "Remember Cathy?"

Frank squatted down so that he was level with Cathy. He looked at her for a long time as if he was trying to see something in her eyes. He slowly offered his big hand to her.

"Hello, Cathy."

Cathy wasn't sure what to do with his hand, so she offered him hers and he held it gently.

He looked at her for a few more seconds and then Aunt Kay cleared her throat.

"Let's get a move on, kids!"

They arrived at the Larion house and Aunt Kay showed them to their room. They were going to be staying for a month before making their way to Stratford where Rita lived.

The room was clean, the floors were gleaming, and the bedding smelled like bleach. There wasn't a single speck of dust, and you could almost see your reflection in the shiny surface of the dresser.

"Isn't this a lovely room, Cathy-o?" Rita said as she quickly put their few things away. "Your Aunt Kay is the cleanest woman I know. Everywhere she goes, she has a rag in one hand and a bottle of bleach in the other." She laughed as she shut the wardrobe door. "You're going to love it here, Hun. Brantford is a beautiful city, and I'm going to show you the places I lived, where I worked, and the parks and the restaurants I loved. Did you know I lived here during the war, and I worked in a factory making parts for airplanes?" Cathy didn't know anything about the war, and she didn't understand why her mother lived in Stratford now or why she moved from Brantford. She knew she was born in a place called Hamilton, and she didn't think it was very far from here. She wondered if the man who was her father lived here in Brantford or in Hamilton or maybe in Stratford. She didn't know who he was. Whenever she asked Nana, she would just sort of shrug her shoulders and turn back to whatever task she was doing.

Rita sat Cathy on the bed and put her arms around her. "I love you so much, Cathy. We're going to have lots of fun here with Kay and Frank, you just wait and see." She gave Cathy a quick kiss on the head and then went to find Aunt Kay.

The bed was soft and bouncy and so high off the floor that Cathy could look straight out the big window and onto the street. Cathy opened her purse and took out the compact. She opened it up and looked at the little girl in the mirror. The girl smiled at her and she looked happy. Cathy was glad because she was happy too. She shut the compact, jumped off the bed, and went to see where her mom and Aunt Kay went.

The next four weeks went by in a whirlwind after they fell into a happy, easy routine. Uncle Frank worked almost every day at what Cathy called the "shampoo factory" and Aunt Kay shopped for groceries, cooked, and cleaned the house spick and span. Aunt Kay and her mom spent hours drinking tea, smoking cigarettes, and talking about life down home and how their younger brother Francis was carrying on. They talked in low whispers about how he would start drinking and then come home so mad that he would throw a fit. Papa would send him out of the house on his ear and tell him to go sober up somewhere. Cathy was afraid of Francis, and it seemed like all of her aunts and uncles were too. Even Nana was scared whenever Francis was home and Papa was down in the pit. Cathy was getting sick of hearing about that stupid article, Francis, and hoped her mom and aunt would change the subject.

In the afternoons, when it got too hot to sit in the kitchen her mom and aunt would take Cathy to the park and buy her ice cream, then they would come home and start preparing supper for Uncle Frank.

One weekend they decided to plan a barbecue, and Cathy had fun helping plan the menu and getting the groceries with her mom and aunt. She was really excited because her mother told her that Uncle Doug and his wife, Aunt Elsie, were coming down from Stratford. Cathy knew that Uncle Doug was one of her mother's brothers; he was second in line and Aunt Kay came third.

Elsie Sardine was born and raised in a place called the West Indies where she had lived with her parents and her brothers and sisters. Cathy heard that Aunt Elsie "came from money" and that she had servants who had to do whatever she told them to do because her father was the Magistrate. Cathy thought it was hard to understand Aunt Elsie when she talked because she had a funny sing-song island accent. Cathy met Uncle Doug and Aunt Elsie for the first time when they came to Cape Breton for their honeymoon. They were really nice to her then and she was excited that they were coming to the barbecue.

It was a hot day, and everyone was wearing shorts, blouses and white cotton shirts. Uncle Frank wasn't even wearing a shirt, and he was being so silly making faces that everyone kept laughing every time he came in from barbecuing outside. Her mom was wearing her short shorts with a strapless halter top. Cathy loved her top because it had white stars all over it and it was so short that it showed her stomach. Cathy was so proud that her mom was the prettiest one in the room; she could hardly believe that she was her mother.

All the windows and the doors in the house were open to let the warm breeze in. There was music playing and the house was full and everyone was excited to have a little party to celebrate the summer. There was Uncle Frank and Aunt Kay, Uncle Doug and Aunt Elsie, and a pretty lady with glasses named Rose Marie. Her mother was waiting anxiously because her new boyfriend, a man named Walter, was supposed to arrive any minute. Cathy kept hearing everyone say his last name and to her it sounded like "Glass Whiskey".

Uncle Frank's brother, Reg Larion, was also there. He and Uncle Frank had been out at the farmer's market earlier that morning to buy steak, fresh vegetables and bread. They were drinking cold beer at the kitchen table and telling stories of their days in the military to Aunt Kay, her mom, and Uncle Doug and Aunt Elsie. Uncle Frank had been in the army and Reg had been in the navy and the two of them were making everyone laugh hysterically about some story from the good old days during the war.

There was a knock at the door, and when Rita rushed to the door to let Walter in, the men at the table stopped laughing. Frank stood up and went to the door to greet Walter.

"Walter. Thanks for coming," Frank said holding out his hand.

"Thanks for having me, Frank. Good to see you." Walter smiled slightly as he shook hands with Frank.

"Well, I should get going, everyone. I've got some work to do around the house and I can't sit around here all day." Reg drained his beer bottle and slapped his brother affectionately on the back as he walked towards the door.

"Walter." Reg nodded in Walter's direction.

"Reg." Walter barely nodded back at Reg before he stepped to Rita's side.

Rita quickly took Walter's hand and led him out of the kitchen and into the living room.

"See you, folks. Have a great day." Reg waved as he went out the door, letting it slam behind him.

Kay and Frank looked at each other with wide eyes. Kay shrugged her shoulders and herded Doug and Elsie into the living room. Frank busied himself getting everyone drinks.

They all settled down in the living room, and, as usual, the waxed wooden floor was shining and it felt cool on Cathy's bare legs when she sat down. Uncle Frank passed out the drinks and offered everyone a cigarette. He started telling another story about the war, and in no time they were all laughing again and clinking glasses with each other.

Aunt Kay got her camera out and was trying to get everyone to look in her direction long enough to take a picture, but they all just kept lighting cigarettes, getting each other more drinks, and laughing their heads off.

"OK, gang! Let's get it together. I want to take some photographs. Frank, you get in the back and Dougie, would you stop talking for two seconds so I can take your picture?"

Uncle Doug sat behind Aunt Elsie and started squeezing her shoulders and blowing in her ear.

"Oh, Douglas! You stop that right now!" Aunt Elsie giggled.

"Alright gals, show us those gams!" laughed Aunt Kay as she continued to try to get control.

Cathy loved posing for the pictures. Aunt Kay had cut her long bangs for her and had her dressed up in a little white dress with flowers all over it and cute bows on the shoulders. That meant she had three dresses now: one yellow, one white, and one blue. She had white ankle socks and a new pair of white dress shoes. While Aunt Kay took the pictures, Cathy tried to sit on her mom's lap, but Walter kept putting his arms around Rita and not leaving any space for Cathy, so she sat back down on the floor. Frank took the camera from his wife so that Kay could be in the pictures too. Kay picked Cathy up from the floor and put her in her lap. She wrapped her arms around her and kissed the back of her neck and tickled her. Cathy was giggling and squirming and loving every second of it.

When supper was ready, the group moved outside to sit in the backyard to eat. Once the meal was done and the guests were full, it finally started to cool down and a little breeze blew through the yard. The laughter died down as the grown-ups lit their cigarettes, got comfortable in their lawn chairs, and smiled quietly to each other as the sun slowly set.

Cathy was curled up beside Aunt Kay on the lounge chair, and her eyes were getting heavy. She closed them while Aunt Kay put her arms around her and kept her warm in the cool evening air. She could hear the murmur of their talk, a quiet giggle here and there, and then finally goodbyes as they got up to pack their things and head home.

Uncle Frank picked her up out of Aunt Kay's arms and put her over his shoulder. She nuzzled her face into his neck and wrapped her arms around him. She could smell cigarette smoke, beer, and the faint scent of his cologne. He carried her to the spare room, gently put her down in the big soft bed, and pulled the blankets up over her. He smoothed her hair back out of her face and put his big hand on her little shoulder and held it there. His hand made her feel all warm and cozy and protected. He gently squeezed her shoulder and leaned down and kissed her cheek. Just before Cathy fell asleep, she thought of her friend, and she knew if she opened her compact and looked in the mirror, her friend would look happy, content, and loved.

The Gorman Family

CHAPTER SIX

Stratford-Early September 1955

The train ride wasn't nearly as long as the one they took from Sydney to Brantford, and after only a few hours of looking out the window at all the little towns and the fields going by, they arrived in Stratford. It was evening, but the sun hadn't set yet and the breeze was warm and fresh.

Rita picked up the two suitcases and led Cathy down onto the platform. The station was large, and there were big cars lined up and down the street with people waiting for their friends and family to come off the train. Cathy wondered if someone would be there waiting for them, like Uncle Frank and Aunt Kay had in Brantford, but Rita started walking away from the train station towards the busy road.

Cathy would always remember how much fun it was staying at Aunt Kay's house, and how much she grew to love Aunt Kay and Uncle Frank, but she was really looking forward to starting their new life in Stratford; this was the adventure her mom told her about. Suddenly, with a surge of excitement, she ran to catch up to her mother.

They walked and walked, and after a while Cathy's feet were getting tired. She reached out to hold her mother's hand, but Rita had to carry both their suitcases and her purse and wasn't able to take Cathy's outstretched hand. They kept walking and Rita had to stop and rest a lot, but every time they stopped, she smiled at Cathy, blew the hair out of her eyes, and said, "It won't be long now, Cathy-o, just a few more blocks." She stood up, took hold of the two suitcases, and started back up the road. Cathy walked as fast as she could but was having a hard time keeping up.

They finally arrived at the house. Cathy didn't know much about where they were going to live, but she pictured a little house with a little yard and a nice cozy kitchen with a wood stove, just like at Nana's. She was surprised when her mother reached the front door and knocked. Cathy thought her mother would just get her key and open the door for them. Instead she knocked on the door again and they waited. After a few minutes, the door opened and there stood a lady who smiled and said, "Hello Rita!

I'm glad you made it before it got dark." She opened the door to let them in and took the suitcases from Rita.

"Oh thank you, Mrs. Gorman," Rita sighed with relief. "My arms are killing me. I couldn't hold those suitcases one more minute. Lucky for us the train leaving Brantford was on time and it didn't take long to get to Stratford at all."

"And you must be little Cathy? I've heard all about you, my dear! Your mother has been talking about you non-stop since she moved here in June." Mrs. Gorman took Cathy's hand and led her into the kitchen. "Let me just get you a nice cold glass of milk, and you can sit right here and rest your little legs," she said as she made her way over to the fridge.

"Thanks again, Mrs. Gorman. My Cathy must be exhausted after our walk from the station, and I really should get her to bed as soon as possible," said Rita.

Cathy drank her milk slowly and wondered where her bed might be, and although Mrs. Gorman seemed really nice, she was still surprised that she and her mom were going to live with her and not in their very own house, the way she had hoped.

Rita took Cathy up the stairs and turned left into a little bedroom. There was one bed in the middle of the room, a nightstand with a washbasin on it, and a wardrobe in the far corner. Rita helped Cathy take off her dress and her sandals and got her nighty out of the blue suitcase. She dressed her and then led her to the bathroom down the hall where she went to the toilet and brushed her teeth. Cathy padded back down the hallway in her bare feet, and as they got back into the room, Rita picked her up and laid her on the bed.

"You are quite a little girl, Cathy-o. You were such an angel on the train and everyone kept asking me where I got such a beautiful little girl. Imagine—only five years old, and traveling all the way from Nova Scotia to Brantford and then to Stratford!" She pulled her daughter close to her, buried her face into Cathy's neck, and hugged her tight. Cathy put her arms around her mother's neck and squeezed; it felt so good, she never wanted to let go. After a few moments, Rita stood up, pulled the blankets up to Cathy's chin, and said,

"Nighty night, don't let the bedbugs bite!" She walked over to the lamp and turned it off and as she got to the door, Cathy asked, "Where are you going to sleep, Mommy?"

Rita answered, "With you, of course. Good night, Hun." And closing the door, she left Cathy in the darkness and strangeness of their new room.

The next morning, Cathy awoke and at first didn't know where she was. Normally Papa's rooster would be crowing by now, but instead she heard someone gently snoring. She slowly raised herself up and looked beside her and there was her mother curled up on her side with the blanket over her head. Cathy felt so warm and cozy in the bed with her mom, she wished they could stay under the blankets all day. After a few moments, Rita turned over, opened her eyes, and smiled tiredly at Cathy.

"Good morning, Sunshine. Let's get up and start the day. It's your first day of school and I've got something exciting to show you downstairs." She sat up, opened the blankets, put on her housecoat, and went to the door.

Cathy jumped out of bed, and passing the mirror on the way out of the bedroom, she saw the little girl. The little girl looked tired and her hair was sticking up, but she looked excited and she smiled at Cathy. Cathy smiled back and waved and then ran out the door to follow her mom down the stairs and into the kitchen.

She was surprised to see that there was a girl sitting at the table eating her breakfast.

"Hi," she said. "My name's Ann. I'm six. My mom told me you would be here when I got up. Do you know that we're going to school together today?"

Cathy was very surprised because her mother didn't tell her that there would be a girl her own age to play with. Tucked into the table was a highchair with another little girl. She was much younger than Ann, but was she ever cute!

"That's my sister, Maureen. She's only two, but we can play with her if we're really gentle," said Ann.

Cathy walked slowly over to the little girl, reached out her hand, and gently touched her rosy chubby cheek.

"Hi, Maureen," she said very quietly and sweetly. She loved little babies so much! There was always a baby cousin or neighbour at Nana's, and Cathy often got to change their diapers and feed them. But best of all, Nana let her sit in her rocking chair and hold the little darlins until they fell asleep.

"OK girls! Let's eat breakfast and then go upstairs and get ready for your big day." Rita smiled as she went to put bread in the toaster.

Rita and Susan Wrenn at 28 Brant Street

CHAPTER SEVEN

Stratford-Winter 1956

Cathy loved her new life in Ontario with her mom, and although she thought about Nana, Janey, and Marlene all the time, she couldn't help but wonder if this was where she really belonged; with Ann, Mrs. Gorman, and most especially, with her mom.

Every morning, her mother walked Cathy and Ann to St. Joseph's Catholic School. Cathy loved her class and loved her teacher and, best of all, she loved Ann. She loved how Ann waited for her after school, and how they walked home together back to Mrs. Gorman's. After they had their milk and cookies the girls would run up the stairs to Ann's room and play with her dolls. Rita would come home after work, help Mrs. Gorman fix supper, and they would all eat together at the kitchen table.

One day in the middle of winter, Cathy and Ann arrived home after school. The cold, damp wind blew in as they shut the door quickly behind them. After taking off their coats and boots, the girls went into the kitchen and found Rita and Mrs. Gorman sitting at the table having a cup of tea. Both women looked up at the girls with worried expressions on their faces.

"Well girls, we have some good news and some bad news," Rita said as she stood up and went over to Cathy and squatted down in front of her. "The good news is, is that little Maureen has grown into a big girl! She's so big, that she gets to have her own bed in her own room."

The girls looked at each other and smiled because they knew Maureen was getting way too big for her crib; just the other day they caught her trying to climb out of it after her nap. She wanted to find Cathy and Ann so she could play with their doll's. She was what Nana would call a "going concern."

Then Cathy looked at her mother and asked quietly, "What's the bad news, Mommy?"

"The bad news, is that we have to let Maureen have our room." She tried her best to smile. "So we're going to find a new place to live."

Ann looked puzzled, but then said in an excited voice, "You don't have to find a new place. Cathy can stay with me in my room." Her face lit up with the idea of the two friends staying in the same room.

"Aw, Hun, thanks for the thought, but then where would I sleep?" Rita asked.

"Oh," said Ann as her face fell. She looked at Cathy. Cathy looked back at Ann and then looked at her mom and finally at Mrs. Gorman. She was too shy to say anything, but she could feel her throat tightening and feel the prickles behind her eyes as the tears threatened to fall.

She didn't want to leave the little house. They had only been there for a few months and they were so happy, and Mrs. Gorman and Ann were so nice. Where would they go? Would they go back to Nova Scotia? Who would play with little Maureen?

"Don't worry, my dear," Mrs. Gorman said as she went to Cathy and put her hand on her shoulder. "I have the name of a woman who has agreed to take you in. Her name is Mrs. Wrenn, and she lives over by the train station. She has a little boy and a little girl, and she said you can move in right away." Mrs. Gorman looked at Rita and then quickly looked down at the floor.

Rita cleared her throat and said, "Cathy, we have to leave this weekend. But listen Hun, it's going to be OK, and I don't want you to be sad because it will be another fun adventure, and I'm sure we'll love living with the Wrenns."

She stood up and tried to smooth the wrinkles out of her skirt. She looked like she didn't know what else to say, so she glanced over at Mrs. Gorman.

"Now girls, go run upstairs and play with your dolls while Rita and I finish our tea," said Mrs. Gorman.

Rita tucked a curl of black hair behind her ear, went back to the table, and with a sigh reached for her cold cup of tea.

Rita and Cathy set out from Mrs. Gorman's house two days later. It was a cold and dark evening, and the snow was coming down heavily. Rita and Cathy were all packed with their coats on, but it took forever to finally get going because Cathy and Ann couldn't stop crying and hugging each other in the front hallway. Ann gave Cathy one of her favourite dolls and told her that they would still see each other at school, and although they couldn't walk home together anymore, they could still play at recess. Cathy just nodded and wiped the tears from her cheeks. She took the doll with one hand and picked up her little blue suitcase with the other.

As Cathy looked through fresh tears at Ann, she remembered how Mrs. Gorman took care of her and Ann when they had the measles together last fall, and how Mrs. Gorman would let Cathy sit in Ann's room when she had tummy aches. Ann often had tummy aches and had to miss school every couple weeks or so. Cathy would sit at her bedside and hold her hand and wait for when Ann would feel better, so they could go outside and play. Cathy would always remember that Ann Gorman was her first real friend.

Six years later, Cathy's heart would break when she found out that Ann had died of kidney failure just before her twelfth birthday.

Rita and Cathy trudged through the deep snow and pulled their coats tight. They had no extra money for a taxi, so they walked the almost two miles back towards the train station they had arrived at only five months earlier. They went all the way down Nile Street, and then turned left on Brant Street. They walked halfway up and stopped at number 28.

The house was dark; not even a porch light on. Rita walked up the two sagging wooden steps and just before she reached out to knock on the door, a sudden high-pitched whistle sounded in the still night air. It was a train, and it was whistling and screeching its brakes as it pulled into the station. Cathy had no idea they were so close to the train station. How could people sleep with all that racket?

The porch light suddenly went on, and Cathy could see that the house was made of brownish brick. In the dim light it looked shabby and not well-taken care of. Cathy couldn't tell, but maybe all of the houses on the street looked the same.

The door opened slightly and a squinty-eyed face appeared. The woman opened the door all the way and stood in the dimness of the porch light.

"Hummph…I expected you an hour ago. It's a little late to be knocking on someone's door isn't it?" she muttered in a thick British accent while she peered out from behind her smudged glasses.

Mrs. Wrenn looked to be about four feet ten inches tall. She was very fat with thick legs and small hands and feet. She was cross-eyed and her glasses were as thick as her legs. She had greasy black hair, streaked with grey and parted on the side, flattened down by a barrette. She was wearing a stained grey house dress with thick black shoes tied up with laces. Her mouth was pinched, and it looked like she was sucking on a humbug or a carrot or something.

"Who's this?" Cathy heard a man say in a low voice. He had come up behind Mrs. Wrenn and put his hands on her shoulders. She was so short that her head only came up to the lower part of his chest. This must be her husband, Mr. Wrenn, thought Cathy; but he was her complete opposite. He was very tall and thin and, unlike his wife, had a kindly face.

"It's that Rita Barron woman and her kid that I was telling you about," Mrs. Wrenn answered as she shrugged his hands off her shoulders. "They're going to be staying up in the room for awhile."

"Shall we let them in out of the cold, Dear?" he asked as he reached around her and gestured for Rita and Cathy to come in.

They stepped into the front hall as Mrs. Wrenn closed the door behind them. It was dark and for some reason they didn't have the hall light on either, although there was a flickering light coming from the living room where they must have had a TV.

"You'll have to be quiet, my children are in their beds fast asleep," Mrs. Wrenn whispered. She looked at Rita as if to say, *and so should your kid*. She didn't smile or act nice or offer to take their things. She just stood there peering at them in the half dark. Why didn't she turn the light on for God's sake?

As Rita helped Cathy take off her snow covered coat and her wet boots, Cathy heard a noise coming from the room with the TV.

"What's that noise?" she whispered to her mother.

"It's the bird cage in the corner over there," answered Mrs. Wrenn as she glanced over toward the TV room.

Cathy had never heard such a noise. She was amazed by the high-pitched squeaking and chirping sounds, and she asked, "How many birds are there?"

Mrs. Wrenn looked at her and, starting to look irritated, she said, "There's one bird."

The bird was making so much noise that Cathy couldn't believe there was only one.

"How many birds?" she asked again.

"What's the matter with you?" Mrs. Wrenn raised her voice, "I told you, ONE bird!"

Cathy's eyes grew wide. She closed her mouth, took a step towards her mother and didn't say another word. She wanted to cry because she couldn't believe that someone would talk so mean to her.

All of her life, Cathy was treated gently by Nana and her aunts and uncles, and Papa loved her so much he never raised his voice at her the way he would to the other kids.

She was always a good girl. She was never bad or saucy or anything. She always felt like the darling of the family, not only because she was their first grandchild, but also because she was Rita's daughter.

Cathy knew her mom was Nana and Papa's favourite daughter; she was the apple of their eye. They were so proud of her and told everyone how beautiful and smart she was, and how she went up to Ontario to make a better life for herself and how she would always send money to help with the rest of her nine brothers and sisters.

So, of course, Cathy was their favourite too; they loved her more than anything. Thinking about Nana and Papa all of a sudden made Cathy's throat tighten and her eyes prickle with tears. She took another step closer to her mother and tried to hide her face in her rough woolen coat.

Mrs. Wrenn looked at Cathy and then at Rita. She shook her head and tisk-tisked under her breath. She led them up the stairs, past the second floor to another, smaller set of stairs that led up to their room under the slanted roof.

The room was small and the ceiling was low. There was one small window on the left wall, and it was so high up that you couldn't really see out of it. On the right wall there was a double bed with a sagging mattress and a brown bedspread draped over top. The bed had a brass headboard, but it was rusty, dull, and cold looking. There was a dresser with a mirror attached to it against the wall, and another small window just above the bed. In the main part of the room, on the far side, there was a counter with a hotplate and a few cups and saucers stacked on one shelf. The dishes looked chipped and stained. There was no bathroom, no sitting room, and no kitchen. Mrs. Wrenn said that Rita and Cathy would have to use the bathroom downstairs on the second floor, and she'd rather them not use it too late at night or too early in the morning. She also said that they could use the kitchen, but they were expected to buy their own groceries, do their own dishes, and make sure the kitchen was spotless before they left it.

The most curious thing about the room was the single bed sitting in the middle of what would have been the living area. There was a bed frame with no headboard or footboard, just a box spring and a stained mattress on top. Cathy wondered if this was supposed to be their sofa because after looking around at the room there was no real place to sit.

"Now, that's Kenny's bed, and I'm keeping it for him until he's ready for it," Mrs. Wrenn said as she gestured to the single bed. "I want it kept clean for him, so I would thank you not to sit on it."

Don't sit on it? Cathy thought. Where can we sit then?

As if Mrs. Wrenn could hear her thoughts, she said, "You can sit on your own bed or at the table over there."

Over on the left-hand wall under the little window there was a grey Formica folding table with two chairs. That's where they would have to sit to eat, drink tea, and do everything else.

Rita thanked Mrs. Wrenn and said that she and Cathy would like to unpack their things now. And, she assured her, they would not sit on Kenny's bed. Mrs. Wrenn squinted at Rita from behind her thick glasses, gave a loud suck to the humbug, and turned and went down the stairs.

Rita looked at Cathy and raised her eyebrows and opened her brown eyes wide, something that Nana would have done, but she didn't say a word.

She walked over to what was now their bedroom. There was no door, and the bed was just sort of pushed against the wall, so not really a room at all.

Just as Rita and Cathy started to unpack their suitcases, a loud shrill shriek made them both jump out of their skins. It was the train pulling into the station. Once again Cathy thought, how the heck are we going to get used to that sound?

After the train blasted its whistle for the last time, they silently put their few belongings in the drawers of the dresser, and then got their nighties on. They both crept down the stairs hoping that it wasn't too late to use the bathroom, climbed the stairs back up again, and after shutting off the light, got into the bed.

Cathy had to scooch across the bed to get to her side beside the wall, but as she sat up to get the doll Ann gave her, she hit her head on the slanted ceiling. It really hurt and she wanted to cry, but her mother had her back to her while she finished her prayers and blessed herself. She knew her mother was very tired and just wanted to go to sleep, so Cathy didn't let on about hitting her head. She would have to be careful not to sit up in the night or she would hit it again.

Cathy realized that she and her mom would once again be sharing a bed, but she didn't mind because then she got to snuggle up behind her mother's back.

Rita reached behind her and took Cathy's little hand, gave it a squeeze and said, "Good night, Hun. Don't let the bed bugs bite." She laid down on her right side and pulled the blanket up over her head.

Cathy curled herself up against her mother's back and pulled the blanket over her head too. She hoped there weren't any bed bugs in the thin brown spread, but she couldn't be sure.

Rita

CHAPTER EIGHT

Stratford-Winter 1956

The next morning at sunrise, Rita got out of the bed and went to find the kettle. The apartment was cold and she couldn't find her slippers. She found a pair of socks, put them on, and then went all the way downstairs to the kitchen to find the tap. She took the newspaper from the kitchen table, filled up the kettle, and hiked back up to the attic. She made herself a hot tea on the hotplate; she wanted some toast with it but hadn't bought any groceries yet, and she didn't think she should take any of

Mrs. Wrenn's bread. Instead of breakfast, she drank her tea, lit a cigarette, and started reading the paper. After a while, she looked over at her daughter sleeping in the bed, facing the wall.

As if Cathy could feel her mother's gaze, she slowly opened her eyes, looked out from the blanket, and stared at the wall. It took her a few moments to remember where she was. She reached behind her back for her mother, but only felt a warm space where she had just been sleeping. Cathy turned over and when she saw her mother sitting at the kitchen table with her tea, she smiled. "Good morning, Mommy," she said with a yawn.

"Good morning, Darlin'," Rita said as she came over to sit on the bed. She kissed Cathy's plump cheek and smoothed down her hair. "I have to get ready and get to the Laundry. Don't forget that Mrs. Wrenn will give you breakfast and then you can walk to school with her son, Kenny." She got up to ash her cigarette.

Kenny and his sister, Susan, were the Wrenn's two adopted children. Kenny was a year or two older than Cathy, and Susan was two or three years younger. She hadn't met them yet, but she was hoping they would be nice and would like to play with her. She wondered if Susan had any dolls.

Cathy watched her mother put on the white uniform she wore to the Laundry at the Stratford General Hospital.

Rita sat on the end of the bed to put her nylons on and, looking in the mirror above the dresser, she brushed her hair and applied her red lipstick. She put on her coat and grabbed her purse and gave Cathy another kiss. "I've got to go, Hun. Have a great day at school!" She hurried down the stairs and out the door.

Cathy sat in the bed for another few minutes wishing her mom would have taken her down to the kitchen, but now she was gone and Cathy wasn't exactly sure what to do. Should she wait for Mrs. Wrenn to come and get her, or should she get dressed and go downstairs? She listened to see if she could hear any voices or noises coming from the kitchen down on the main floor. Nothing. She got out of the bed and went to the dresser. If she stood up on her tippy toes, she could see the mirror and the little girl looking back at her.

Cathy wondered how the little girl was feeling about living in this new place. The girl's dark blue eyes were wide open and looked worried. Cathy felt bad for the little girl. She didn't want her to be scared, so she said, "Let's get dressed and go down. Then we can meet Kenny and Susan and see what time we'll be walking to school."

Just as Cathy opened the drawer to get her dress out, she heard a creak at the bottom of the stairway. She listened to see if someone was coming up the stairs. She didn't hear anything else, so she started pulling her dress over her head.

"Bring down the beacon!" Mrs. Wrenn suddenly yelled.

Bring down the beacon? Cathy stopped. What's the beacon? She quickly pulled her dress down over her head and ran around the small room to see where the beacon was. "Can't you hear me? Bring down the beacon!" Mrs. Wrenn yelled again.

Cathy started panicking because she didn't know what the beacon was. She looked at the table and at the counter, but nothing was jumping out at her.

"What are you DOING?" snarled Mrs. Wrenn as she made her way up the stairs. She flew into the room, looked at Cathy, looked at Kenny's bed and said, "Are you blind? The beacon's right there!"

There on Kenny's stained mattress was a newspaper. Mrs. Wrenn snatched it off the bed. "Your mother must have stolen it from the kitchen. Next time she should wait until we've at least finished it," she said as she stomped back down the stairs.

Cathy was sure her mom only meant to borrow it, not steal it. And how was Cathy supposed to know that Stratford's newspaper was called *The Beacon Herald*?

Her heart was pounding like a trip hammer. She wished her mom was there. The last thing she wanted to do was go downstairs now. She looked around hoping there was some way to escape. She saw her bed and thought about jumping back in and pulling the blankets over her head. But the thought of Mrs. Wrenn coming back up the stairs made her think better of it, so she went down the stairs to the main floor.

She found the kitchen and stood in the doorway.

Mrs. Wrenn was at the counter pouring cereal into three bowls. Kenny and Susan were at the table with a glass of milk in front of each of them.

"Hi!" Kenny said as he took a drink of his milk.

"Hi," answered Cathy.

She looked at Susan. "Hi. I'm Cathy Barron."

Susan had a doll in the chair beside her and she picked it up and made its hand wave at Cathy.

"My dolly's name is Moira. She's happy to meet you."

Cathy smiled and thought about going to get her doll to show Susan, but Mrs. Wrenn cleared her throat and pointed her eyes to the empty chair at the table.

"Sit there," she said as she set the bowls at each place.

Cathy sat down and looked at the bowl. She saw tiny little brown things floating in about an inch of milk. She didn't know what they were, but found her spoon and took a bite. It tasted awful! The little things were hard and it felt like she had gravel in her mouth. She looked at Kenny and Susan's bowls. They had the same yucky looking stuff, but their bowls were full of milk and she noticed the brown things were softening up and getting puffy.

"C-could I please have some more milk for my cereal?" she asked quietly. She could hardly get the words out of her mouth because she was afraid to ask, but she knew she couldn't eat the gravel the way it was.

"Your mother will have to get milk when she gets her groceries. I don't have any more milk for you. You'll have to make do with what you have."

Cathy looked down at her bowl and started to eat again. She almost gagged at the gritty feel of the cereal in her mouth. She found out later that it was called Grape-Nuts.

Mrs. Wrenn brought hot toast over to Kenny and Susan and a jar of jelly. Cathy was relieved because the jam would help her get the cereal down. She waited for Mrs. Wrenn to give her a piece too, but she just sat at the table and started eating her breakfast. Hot toast with jam was not offered to Cathy.

Cathy was disappointed when she found out that she would not be walking to school with Kenny, after all. The Wrenn

family was Protestant, so Kenny went to Anne Hathaway Public
School and because Cathy was a Catholic, she went to St Joseph's.
The two schools were far away from each other, so Mrs. Wrenn
told Cathy she would have to walk by herself. Susan would stay at
home because she wasn't old enough to go to school yet.

Mr. Wrenn, who had come into the kitchen while the
children were finishing their breakfast, said that he could walk
Cathy to school. Mrs. Wrenn told him not to trouble himself.
Cathy had been going to the same school since September and
she was sure she could figure out how to get there. Mr. Wrenn
said in his low voice, "Yes dear, but we're on the opposite side
of town from where she used to live and she might get herself
all turned around."

"Suit yourself, but don't be late for work."

Mr. Wrenn walked Cathy to school that first day, but after
that, Mrs. Wrenn insisted that Cathy could make her own way
to school.

Cathy was so happy to be back in her kindergarten class with
her teacher and the little friends she'd made, but the best part
of the day was spending recess with Ann. Near the end of the
day, she started to feel nervous because although she had just
walked from the Wrenn's house that morning, she didn't exactly
know how to retrace her steps. After saying goodbye to Ann,
she started walking alone down Nile Street, and although she
was unsure of herself at first, she saw the train station, crossed
the tracks, and finally managed to get back to 28 Brant Street.

When Cathy climbed the two wooden steps and reached the
front door, she wondered if she should knock or go right in.

She reached for the door handle and tried to pull the latch down with her thumb, but it wouldn't move. She held on to the handle with one hand and pressed down on the latch with the other hand using all her weight, but it still didn't move. It was locked. Not sure what to do, she waited a minute to see if someone would open the door. No one did, so she had to knock. Mrs. Wrenn whipped the door open as if she had been standing on the other side the whole time.

"Why didn't you just come in?" she said in an irritated voice.

"The door was locked," Cathy said. "I tried to get the latch down but…"

"It's not locked for pity's sake! Just get in, it's freezing outside!"

Cathy took off her coat and boots and before she made her way upstairs to see if her mom was home, Susan came running out of the living room where the bird cage and the TV were.

"Want to come and watch *The Three Stooges*?" she asked as she waved her doll's hand at Cathy.

"OK!" Cathy followed Susan into the living room where Kenny was sitting on the floor in front of the TV.

Cathy and Susan sat down beside him and together they watched *The Three Stooges* until they heard a knock at the door.

"Oh, for pity's sake! The door isn't locked!" huffed Mrs. Wrenn as she came out of the kitchen and went into the hall to open the door for Rita.

Cathy jumped up and ran into the hall. She was so happy to see her mom, and as soon as she took her coat and boots off, Cathy followed her up the two sets of stairs to their room. "How was your day, Hun?" Rita asked Cathy as she sat at the table and lit a cigarette.

"Oh, Mommy!" Cathy whispered. "Mrs. Wrenn said that you stole her newspaper, then she gave me gravel for breakfast, and she wouldn't give me any more milk. And then she wanted me to walk to school by myself, and she locked me out of the house when I tried to get in!" After Cathy told her everything, she knew her mother would march right down those stairs and tell Mrs. Wrenn off.

But instead Rita stubbed out her cigarette and started rubbing her feet.

"Oh, Hun. It was such a long day at the Laundry. My feet are paining like you wouldn't believe. Can you take that kettle and run down and get me some water? I have to soak my feet and cut off these calluses, or I won't be able to stand tomorrow."

Cathy was just about to tell her mom how she had to walk home all by herself and how she almost got lost, but her mom lit another cigarette and leaned her head against the wall. She closed her eyes while she exhaled a long stream of smoke.

Cathy knew how much her mom's feet hurt after a long day at the Laundry, so she got the kettle and made her way quietly down the stairs.

Walter "Glass Whiskey"

CHAPTER NINE

Stratford-Spring 1956

Life at Mrs. Wrenn's was cold, dark, and unfriendly. Rita woke up at dawn every morning, quickly had her toast and tea, and went off to the Laundry. Cathy got ready by herself, went down for breakfast with Kenny and Susan, and then went off to school without anyone to walk with. At night when Rita finally got home, they stayed up in their room under the slanted roof of the attic. They made soup on the hotplate and toast on an old wire hanger they had bent in half. They couldn't sit on Kenny's bed, so they sat at the kitchen table, and while Rita smoked, Cathy used her pencils and made drawings on old brown paper bags they kept from the grocery store.

Rita didn't usually get home from the Laundry until a few hours after Cathy got home from school, and Mrs. Wrenn didn't like the idea of Cathy roaming around the house doing whatever she wanted, so the women agreed that Mrs. Wrenn would babysit Cathy when Rita was out. Mrs. Wrenn said that if she was going to have to take care of Cathy, she would charge Rita an extra $10 per week besides the rent she already paid.

A few days earlier when Cathy went down to breakfast, Mrs. Wrenn sat at the table and went over the rules of the house that she had for Cathy. She had come up with a new rule, and she told Cathy that she could no longer wear her underpants to bed. Cathy didn't understand what was wrong with wearing her underpants to bed and she didn't think she had to listen to Mrs. Wrenn, but when Cathy told her mother about the new rule, Rita told her to do what she was told. Rita didn't want to make Mrs. Wrenn mad because she was worried about being kicked out of the house, and she didn't know where else to go.

One morning, after Rita left for work and Cathy was still lying in bed, she heard a creak on the stairs. She held her breath because she knew Mrs. Wrenn was there listening to see if Cathy was up yet. Cathy's heart started pounding because she knew she had her underpants on. When she got her nighty on the night before, she thought for a second about the new rule, but she just shrugged and thought, how was Mrs. Wrenn going to find out whether she had underpants on or not? So she kept them on and went to sleep. Besides, she hated the feeling of not wearing underpants; it made her feel cold and uncovered.

Cathy held her breath and didn't move because Mrs. Wrenn had started creeping up the stairs. Before she knew it, Mrs. Wrenn was beside the bed, standing over her. She grabbed the blanket and pulled it back. Cathy's nighty was cinched up to her hips and Mrs. Wrenn could plainly see that she had her underpants on.

"Oh, you bad little girl! I TOLD you to take those underpants off at night, and here you are going against my rules and wearing them anyway!" She leaned in close to Cathy's face. Cathy pushed herself back against her pillow as far as she could, but Mrs. Wrenn's breath was hot and sour in her face.

"You better start doing what I tell you to do, or you and your mother will be out of here so fast it'll make your head spin!" She threw the covers back on top of Cathy and looked over at the table.

"I see your mother left your breakfast for you, so there's no need for you to come down to our kitchen this morning," she said as she stomped back down the stairs.

Cathy slowly pulled the blanket back, pulled her nighty down and sat with her little legs dangling over the bed. She didn't know what to think. She wished her mother was there to stop Mrs. Wrenn from coming up the stairs and being so mean to her. She was sure that if her mother was there with her, Mrs. Wrenn wouldn't carry on like this.

She stepped over to the mirror and as soon as she saw her friend's shocked and sad expression, she burst into tears. She couldn't help herself. She felt so violated, so alone, and now her poor little friend was bawling her eyes out too. She reached out and tried to brush her friend's tears away. Then she rubbed her own eyes until her tears stopped. She looked at the reflection and took a shuddering breath and let out a big sigh. She moved away from the mirror and looked over at the table.

There was half a cup of cold tea and a plate with a crust of toast with a bit of marmalade on it. She sat and drank the tea and ate the toast. Her eyes were sore and tired and she just wanted to crawl right back into bed, but she knew Mrs. Wrenn would call her from downstairs, and she just couldn't bear to hear her voice. So she quickly got dressed, picked up her school bag, and went down the stairs and out the front door.

On her way to school, she thought about her life and how miserable she felt. When her mom told her that they would be happy in Ontario, she really believed it. She had thought that they were going to live in a cute house and be a family. She had imagined that her mother would be home waiting for her every day after school, that she would make them a nice supper and they would sit together and talk about their day.

She had imagined her mother would bathe her at night, and read her a story while she brushed her hair. She so desperately wanted to love her mother and be like a normal child in a happy home, like at the Gorman's, but instead her mom was at work all the time, she never cooked, (she couldn't since they didn't have a kitchen), and she didn't bathe her. Mrs. Wrenn told her to have a bath once every couple of days but scolded her if she used too much water. No one ever washed her back or made sure the shampoo was out of her hair. No one dried her off or made sure she brushed her teeth. She felt so lonely, so sad and embarrassed. She cried all the way to school, but just before she walked through the doors, she wiped away her tears and tried to act as normal as she could.

When she got home that evening, she went into the living room to find Kenny and Susan. They were in their usual spots, watching *The Three Stooges* and laughing their heads off. Cathy was cold and tired and didn't feel like laughing, so she just curled up on the couch and watched the flicker of the TV.

She had formed a new habit of sticking her thumb in her mouth and nibbling on the skin around the sides of her nail. Her mother told her to stop doing it because her thumb would get sore. Cathy tried hard to stop, but sometimes, when she wasn't paying attention, she'd find herself absently chewing on her nail.

At that moment, Mrs. Wrenn walked in the living room and saw Cathy with her thumb in her mouth. "Get that thumb out of your mouth! What a dirty thing to do!" she said as she rushed over and swatted Cathy's hand away from her face.

Cathy was so surprised that Mrs. Wrenn would touch her like that that she instinctively pulled her legs in and put her feet up to protect herself.

"Get your feet down young Miss and get upstairs to your room!" Mrs. Wrenn screamed as bits of chewed up carrot flew out of her mouth.

Cathy jumped off the couch, wiping carrot from her face, and ran towards the stairs. She ran up as quickly as she could, but she could hear Mrs. Wrenn yelling after her, "And if I see you with that thumb in your mouth again, you'll be sorry!"

Cathy threw herself on the bed and buried her face into her pillow. She couldn't wait till her mother got home. She knew that as soon as she told her mother that Mrs. Wrenn hit her hand, they would pack up their stuff and find another place to live. Tears of frustration were welling up in her eyes and suddenly she felt very tired.

Cathy must have fallen asleep because when she opened her eyes it was dark in the room, and it was way past the time that her mom would normally have been home from work.

Now that it was spring, the window above the bed was open and Cathy could hear Rita's voice coming up the road, but Cathy could tell she wasn't alone. She heard her mother talking to someone. She crept down the stairs and sat on a step halfway down. She could see her mother's shadow outside the front door and listened to see who her mom was talking to. She heard a man's familiar voice but couldn't remember who it was. She went down the rest of the stairs to the door and opened it and saw her mother with the man's arms around her.

"Hi, Cathy-o," her mother said as she turned her face towards Cathy. "Remember Walter?"

Cathy remembered Walter from last summer when she and Rita stayed at Aunt Kay and Uncle Frank's house in Brantford.

Walter Glaszewski (Cathy pronounced it "Glass Whiskey") had visited a few times when the gang got together. He always had his arms around Rita and seemed to be protecting her from something or keeping her away from someone. When he was around, Rita would smoke more, drink more, and start giggling and being silly. She would sit on his lap and laugh at all his jokes. Cathy didn't think he was that funny and Walter didn't pay much attention to her. He just sort of patted her on the head and then looked beyond her to see where Rita went.

Cathy was surprised to see him here on Mrs. Wrenn's steps. She couldn't imagine that Mrs. Wrenn would like that Rita was hugging and kissing Walter right there for all the neighbours to see.

"Thanks for walking me home, Walter," Rita said as she gave him one last peck on the cheek.

"See ya, Rita. Maybe tomorrow." He turned and waved over his shoulder as he made his way to the sidewalk.

"Maybe, baby!" Rita giggled as she came in the door and closed it behind her. She stumbled as she hung up her coat and was having a hard time getting her shoes off. Mrs. Wrenn came rushing in from the kitchen.

"Who was that?" She asked as she checked to make sure the door was locked.

"That's my boyfriend, Mrs. Wrenn. He's a real sweet guy," Rita said as she winked at Cathy.

"Well don't be asking him to come in this house. The front step is far enough for him," Mrs. Wrenn said as she peered out the window to see Walter's dark shape making its way down the street.

"Don't worry about that Mrs. Wrenn, I know your rules. Come on, Cathy-o, let's head upstairs and I'll tell you all about my day."

Cathy followed her mother up the stairs and was ready to tell her what Mrs. Wrenn did about her underpants that morning and about swatting her thumb out of her mouth.

"Mommy, I can't stand Mrs. Wrenn, you wouldn't believe what she…"

"Hun, can you help me take my nylons off? These feet of mine are killing me and I have to soak them."

As usual, her mother just wanted to have a cigarette and rest her feet. She didn't seem to notice how upset Cathy was. Either she didn't notice or she didn't care. Cathy pulled off her mother's nylons and swallowed back the tears that threatened to fall for the third time that day.

Cathy and Rita

CHAPTER TEN

Stratford-Spring 1956

As miserable as it was living at Mrs. Wrenn's, Cathy couldn't help but look forward to her special day. On April 18, she was going to be 6 years old! At first Cathy thought she would have to have her birthday with Kenny and Susan, and honest to God, she couldn't image anything worse than spending her birthday at the Wrenn's. So when her mother told her they would have a little party for her at Uncle Doug and Aunt Elsie's, Cathy was over the moon.

Uncle Doug and Aunt Elsie lived in a nice two-story brick house at 279 Albert Street. Aunt Elsie was very clean and kept a tidy, organized house. They had a comfortable sofa, a big TV, and a beautiful area rug. She also crocheted doilies in her spare time, and they were on display all over the house: on the sofa, the chairs, the china cabinet, and the coffee table. But the most interesting thing about their house was their golden wall paper. It looked like a cushion or fabric with what looked like buttons all over it. Cathy kept touching the wallpaper to see if it was soft like a pillow and to see if the buttons were real.

Uncle Doug and Aunt Elsie always had food and drink ready for anyone that might drop in. Neighbours and friends always felt welcome and they often gathered around the piano, sang songs and had a few drinks. Cathy couldn't think of a better place to have a party.

On the morning of Cathy's birthday, Rita woke up first. She made tea and toast for the two of them and then gently woke Cathy up. "Good morning, birthday girl. Guess how old you are today?" Rita said as she led her daughter to the kitchen table. "If you guess right, I'll tell you about your big surprise."

"Oh, Mommy, of course I know how old I am. I'm 6! Please tell me what the surprise is!" Cathy begged as Rita smiled behind her tea cup. "I'm so excited I could burst!"

"Alright, alright! Please don't burst! Mrs. Wrenn would have a fit," Rita joked as she moved her tea out of the way. She reached across the kitchen table and took Cathy's hands. "I am going to take you uptown to a professional photographer and he is going to take your picture!"

Cathy had never had a professional picture taken before. She didn't really know what to expect, but it sure sounded fun. "What will I wear?"

"Just you wait and see. Now close your eyes and don't peek," Rita said as she went over to the dresser and pulled out a package wrapped in tissue paper. She put the package into Cathy's hands. "Now open your eyes."

Cathy opened her eyes and the package, and she pulled out a new dress. It was dark blue with a scooped neck and a little belt that buckled in the front. Also in the package was a beautiful crisp white short-sleeved blouse to be worn under the dress.

"Thank you so much! Will I wear it for my portrait?" Cathy asked as she held the dress up against her chest.

"Well of course, silly goose. That's what I bought it for. Do you love it?"

"I love it! I think I'll look like a princess when I have it on."

After they dressed and did their hair, they walked uptown. There was still snow on the ground, but it was mild and everything was turning to slush. Spring was coming; the birds were singing and Cathy was feeling lighter and happier than she had for months.

They arrived at the studio, combed their hair, and straightened their dresses. Cathy got her portrait done first, and then Rita said she wanted one with the two of them. Cathy felt like they were two princesses, sitting on their royal thrones, posing for a great artist.

When they finished, Cathy felt so happy she hugged her mom and even kissed her on the cheek. It had been a while since she'd done that and Rita seemed pleasantly surprised and kissed her back.

When they came out of the studio, Cathy was surprised to see that Uncle Stan, her Aunt Joanie's boyfriend, was standing on the sidewalk waiting for them. He was wearing a grey trench coat and his fedora pushed back on his head showing his blond hair. Underneath his coat, he wore a shirt and tie and perfectly pressed pants. He always had a smile on his tanned, handsome face. He was kind and caring and Cathy loved him.

"Ah Catty, you a beootiful leetle girl," Uncle Stan said with his thick Polish accent. He picked her up and twirled her around and gave her a mighty hug before he set her back down on the sidewalk. "Reeta, you beootiful too!" He said as he took Rita's hands and kissed them one at a time. Rita beamed. Cathy knew her mother loved Uncle Stan too.

Stan Padacz had arrived from Europe only two years earlier. He grew up in Poland and as a young man fought in the war against the Germans. He arrived in Canada and settled in Stratford where he worked at Fischer Bearings and made fast friends with Uncle Mickey. Joanie came up from Cape Breton in early 1956 when she was only seventeen. She first arrived in Brantford to stay with Kay and Frank, and then she went to Stratford to stay with Doug and Elsie. Their youngest brother, Mickey, lived with Doug and Elsie too, and he and Doug made sure to watch out for their little sister.

A young German girl named Alma Seaman worked at the same factory as Mickey and Stan, and all Mickey wanted to do was take her out on a date, but he was too shy and because Alma only spoke German, he thought they'd have a problem. Since Stan could speak German, Mickey begged him to go with him on the date. Stan was not interested in being the third wheel, so Mickey sweetened the deal by getting Joanie to be Stan's date. As soon as Joanie walked into the restaurant, Stan, not knowing she was Mickey's sister, told everyone at the table, "That's the girl I'm going to marry!" And the rest was history. She was such a sweet, kind girl, he couldn't help but fall in love with her right away. They wanted to marry as soon as possible, but Stan being such an old fashioned gentleman, and thirteen years older, insisted that they wait until she was at least 18.

"Madam, you chariot wait for you." Stan opened the door of his car and waited patiently for Cathy and Rita to get in before he gently shut it again, making sure not to catch their dresses. He ran around the other side and got in behind the steering wheel. "Joan send me get you. Catty, you have big day huh? You excite?" He smiled into the rearview mirror as he put the car in gear and drove them to Uncle Doug and Aunt Elsie's.

They arrived at the house on Albert Street and as they were getting out of the car, Aunt Elsie ran down the stairs holding her little black and white dog. Uncle Doug came hobbling after her with a camera in one hand and his cane in the other. Cathy remembered that he had broken his leg a month earlier on St. Patrick's Day.

As usual, there was a big party at Uncle Doug and Aunt Elsie's, and even though it had been a hundred years since the Barrons left Ireland, they turned into full-blooded Irish when they celebrated St. Patrick's Day on March 17.

Cathy remembered how excited she was when her mom let her get dressed in green and go to the party with all of her aunts and uncles. Everyone was there: Uncle Doug and Aunt Elsie, Aunt Joanie and Stan, her mom and Walter, Uncle Mickey and his girlfriend, Alma, and Bobby O'Donnell and his wife. They were dancing and singing, eating and drinking, smoking cigarettes, and playing cards. One of the ladies played all the old Irish songs like "Danny Boy," "When Irish Eyes Are Smiling," and "Harrigan," on the piano. Cathy wasn't sure what happened exactly, but her Uncle Doug must have been carrying on and ended up in the hospital with a broken leg.

The next day, Aunt Elsie went to visit him and along with a pack of cigarettes, she smuggled in a bottle of whiskey for him to put in his tea. He continued to celebrate St. Patrick's Day from his hospital bed.

That night when they arrived back at Mrs. Wrenn's, Cathy was so tired that Rita put her straight to bed. While she was lying there, her mother went to her dresser drawer and took out an envelope.

"Look at this, Cathy," she said as she sat on the bed. "When your Aunt Kay and I came up to Ontario, we missed celebrating St. Patrick's Day with our family in Cape Breton. We were in the Women's Residence and we were so excited when we got this in the mail."

She opened the envelope and handed Cathy the card from inside. It was a St. Patrick's Day card. On the front was a little leprechaun holding a clover and sitting on a stone, on the inside he was marching and saying, "Top O' the Mornin' and the Luck O' the Irish too!"

In Nana's handwriting the card said, "To Rita and Katy, Love Dad and Mom and all."

"Oh, Mommy, that's a nice card that Nana sent you. When did she send it?"

"Well it must be about ten years ago now. I've always kept it because it reminds me of how much I love Mama and Daddy and how proud I am to be Irish. St. Patrick's Day has always been a happy celebration in our family."

She took the card and put it carefully back into the envelope and then leaned over and kissed Cathy on the forehead.

Smiling at that memory, Cathy's mind slowly returned to the present.

"OK, OK! Get in front of Stan's fancy car and move in close. Move! Move!" Doug said.

Everyone said that only Aunt Elsie and Rita could really understand Uncle Doug. Not only did he have a thick Cape Breton Island accent, but he had a high, raspy voice and spoke so fast you didn't have a clue what he was saying. Cathy always just smiled and nodded whenever he asked her a question.

He aimed the camera and they all posed in front of the car while Aunt Elsie held her dog in her arms and Uncle Stan put his arm around Rita's shoulder.

"OK, enough photos! Let's get in the house," said Aunt Elsie as she herded everyone inside.

"Happy birthday, Cathy!" Aunt Joanie said as she rushed in from the kitchen to give Cathy a big hug. "Guess who's here?"

Cathy looked over Aunt Joanie's shoulder and saw Uncle Mickey standing in the doorway smoking a cigarette.

"Happy birthday, sweetie," he said as she ran over for her hug.

Everyone gave Cathy a little something for her birthday. Uncle Doug and Aunt Elsie gave her a new set of crayons and a colouring book, and of course, a little doily. Aunt Joanie and Uncle Stan gave her pretty writing paper and a new pencil, and Uncle Mickey gave her a little glass figurine of a monkey. They sang "Happy Birthday" while she blew out the candles, and then Aunt Joanie cut the cake and gave big pieces out to everyone. Aunt Elsie even gave her ginger ale to "wash it down" and they sat and talked and wished Cathy a happy sixth birthday over and over again. She felt so warm and cozy and loved by everyone, she didn't want the day to end.

That night when they arrived back at the Wrenn's, Cathy looked in the mirror to see how her friend felt about being six years old. The little girl looked a little tired, but she also looked very happy. Cathy was glad. It always made her feel better when the little girl felt as happy as she did.

"Happy birthday, Hun. I hope you had a nice day," her mother said as she tucked her into bed.

"This was pritnear one of the best days I've ever had!" Cathy said as she snuggled under her blankets and closed her eyes.

Doug, Alice and Francis

CHAPTER ELEVEN

Stratford-Spring 1956

After Rita tucked Cathy into bed for the night, she sat down at the kitchen table and lit a cigarette. She thought about Mama and Daddy and how much she missed them. She remembered the summer of 1946; the factory that she and Kay were working in had shut down for a month for maintenance, so the girls took the opportunity to go down home. They were both looking forward to seeing Mama and Daddy and all their sisters and brothers. On the train down, Rita told Kay about her grand idea. She wanted to gather everyone up and get a family portrait done. With so many children, and Rita and Kay living up in Ontario, Rita felt that there may not be many more opportunities to get the whole family together at the same time. Rita loved the portrait the family had done back when the baby, Rosie, was only two or three years old, but she and Kay had been up in Ontario and missed out.

When Rita brought up the idea to her parents, Daddy had thought it was a great idea but Mama had said that she wasn't so sure. She said she had to worry about all the kids and what clothes they had to wear, of all the laundry and mending she would have to do first. She had supposed they would all need to bathe and get their hair washed and brushed and she wondered if she had any extra bows for the girls' hair. Mama remembered that Molly was so cute with her bow a few years ago when they had the photo taken. She loved that photo, but because it was winter they were all wearing coats and, for some reason, the photographer didn't tell them to take them off. She also remembered being disappointed that Rita and Kay weren't there, so she guessed Rita was right to want to get another family photo done.

It was chaotic the morning of the photoshoot with Rita and Kay doing their long hair in pageboy styles, and their sister Alice being grumpy because she didn't understand why they had to get another portrait done.

Alice went on about how much she loved the one from three years earlier. She had worn a cute jacket and a starched white blouse and the little ones were so sweet sitting on Mama and Papa's laps.

"Just because Rita and Kay left to go live the glamorous life in Ontario, doesn't mean the whole family should have to do the photo again," Alice complained to her mother.

It wasn't her fault her sisters took off and left them all for dead. All she really wanted to do was get back to Johnny Ryan. They were to be married at the end of the summer and although she was excited about becoming his wife, she complained that she hadn't been feeling well lately.

"Just the other morning I got sick in the pail," she told her mother. "And no matter how much sleep I get, I always feel tired."

Rita and Alice were busy fighting over the one mirror they had, so Kay and Molly helped Mama get Tussie, Joanie, and Rosie ready. Francis and Mickey were out in the yard, scuffing up their newly shined shoes and Dougie was hiding behind the shed, sneaking a cigarette.

"OK boys and girls, let's get a move on," Papa said as he finished combing his hair back and straightening his tie.

It was a beautiful summer day and they all walked down the tracks towards Glace Bay. The younger boys ran ahead picking up coal from the tracks, and Papa and Dougie were taking long strides trying to keep up with them. Rita and Kay were holding Tussie's hands and swinging her up in the air while singing "Down in Old Southern Texas". They knew Tussie always got a kick out of that song, she was smiling away and trying to learn the words so she could sing along too.

Alice was looking hot and sweaty and walking with her arms crossed over her stomach, not talking to anyone and poor

Mama was bringing up the rear because she had to carry little Rosie. Rosie was wearing Joanie's old shoes, but her feet must have grown because she was crying that her feet were pinched and she couldn't walk on her own. Molly and Joanie were walking quietly enjoying the sunshine and the ocean breeze.

Once they got home after the photo shoot, Mama went to get her new camera. She wanted some photos of her own, and since all the kids looked so nice and their hair was still clean, she thought this would be the best time to do it. Their dog, Bimbo, came bounding towards them from wherever it was that he roamed during the day. Doug caught him and picked him up and let Bimbo lick him all over his face.

"Put him down, Dougie!" Tussie said. "You're going to hurt him."

"Aw c'mon, Toots! He's alright."

Dougie put Bimbo down and started chasing him all over the yard.

"Come here, Bimbo! Come here!" Kay was patting her knees trying to get his attention. Bimbo raced towards her and jumped up against her chest and she fell over. She was laughing her head off when Dougie ran over to help her get up. Mama took a photo, and then she told Tussie and Molly to get in the picture too. Bimbo was panting and running back and forth between everyone and loving all the attention.

"OK, now Francis and Doug, you get together," Mama ordered still holding the camera.

"Alice, come on!" Francis called to his older sister. "You get in too."

Alice stalked over and stood in between them.

"Smile!" said Mama. The boys smiled.

"I've got an announcement," Papa said trying to get all of their attention. "Tomorrow, we'll be getting on the Aspy to Ingonish to visit the family."

Everyone was excited and happy for this unplanned trip. There was nothing better in the world than going to Ingonish. The kids knew that their father was the happiest once they got over Cape Smokey. He had many brothers and sisters and the kids had hundreds of cousins. The Barrons, the Brewers, the Doucettes; anywhere you went, you were bound to run into a relative. "Who do you belong to?" was how everyone greeted each other in Ingonish.

Kay and Rita decided to wear what they thought were very modern. Trousers! They had each bought a pair of trousers just before leaving Brantford and this would be the perfect place to wear them. They had their new shoes, their short sleeved white blouses, and of course their perfectly coiffed hairdos. The two of them made quite a pair.

Rita had tons of cousins but the one she was closest to had always been Marie Barron. Marie and her sister Margie were the daughters of Nana's sister, Bridget. Whenever Daddy brought the kids to visit his family in Ingonish, Rita and Kay always played with Marie and Margie.

They arrived late that afternoon, and Rita and Kay wanted to take more pictures so they could show off their outfits. Grandma Brewer made a big fuss about them wearing men's pants and shook her head every time one of the girls walked by.

"Grandma Brewer! Let's take a photo," Rita said to her grandmother. "You sit here, and Mama you get in here too." She put her arms around both of them and smiled for the camera.

"Now you take my place, Kay," Rita ordered. As soon as the picture was taken, her mother quickly stood up. It was no secret that she wasn't a fan of her mother-in-law. No one really knew what the problem was, but there was always some tension in the air when the two of them were together.

They had a great time visiting all the relatives, going to Ingonish Beach and visiting those who had passed at St. Peter's churchyard. It was sad to say goodbye to everyone, especially for Daddy. He loved Ingonish so much and always got grumpy when they had to head home.

"Daddy, please don't be upset. We had such a nice visit, didn't we?" Rita hugged her father and kissed him on the cheek. He instantly brightened and put his hand under her chin.

"Aw, Rita—my girl. I wish I could have raised you up here. You would have loved it." He gave her a hug. "Where's that camera now? Let's get a picture of just you and me."

They posed with their arms around each other and Rita's heart swelled with how much she loved Daddy and how much she knew he loved her.

"I hope I marry a man just like you, Daddy. I would be the luckiest girl in the world."

He shrugged his shoulders with embarrassment and hid his shy smile behind his cigarette.

Taking a last drag from her cigarette, Rita finalized her plan in her head. Yes, she would take Cathy down home this summer and they would spend two weeks there. She missed the ocean and the cliffs, the fields and her family. It would be good to get out of this room and away from the Laundry for a couple weeks. She just had to see her father again; she needed to feel his love and she needed him to tell her that he was proud of her, and that she did the right thing by taking care of Cathy. Maybe she would ask Doug and Elise if they wanted to go too.

She stubbed out her cigarette in the overflowing ashtray, blessed herself with the holy water she always kept in a jar on the counter, and crawled into bed beside the warm body of her little girl. She smiled to herself and fell fast asleep.

Papa's Chickens

CHAPTER TWELVE

Cape Breton-Summer/Fall/Winter/Spring 1956-1957

Uncle Doug took the train with her and her mother. They were all excited because Rolfe and Aunt Molly just had a brand new baby girl. They named her Molly, but of course they called her Little Molly, and ever since then, Aunt Molly became Big Molly, which was funny, because she was only four feet eleven inches tall.

Cathy stayed with Nana while her mother went up to Dominion with Aunt Molly, Rolfe, and the baby. Cathy,

Marlene, and Janey all slept together in the same bed at Nana and Papa's house, and even though Marlene was only 3 years old and Janey was only 2 years old, the three of them would take off first thing in the morning to go and play.

They would play with the dog and feed Papa's chickens and take turns holding all the kittens that were hanging around. Papa loved animals, and he was always holding a cat or playing with a dog or trying to tame that crazy old rooster.

Uncle Doug was still on his crutches and because Aunt Elsie didn't come down home on this trip, he spent a lot of time up in Ingonish visiting the Barrons and hanging around with his friend Danny McMullin.

At the end of the two weeks, Rita came up from Big Molly's to Woodward Street with her suitcase packed and her traveling clothes on.

"Well Cathy-o, it's time to go," she said as she started getting Cathy's things and putting them into a bag.

"What? Go where?" Cathy said as she watched her mother going back and forth to the dresser.

"Back to Ontario of course. Where did you think?" her mother said. "C'mon on now, help me pack."

"But I thought I was staying here now, with Nana," Cathy said as she started taking her things out of the bag and putting them back into her drawer. "I'm not going back to Ontario."

Rita stopped what she was doing and sat on the bed. "Cathy, you know that we were only here for a visit. You are coming back with me because school is starting soon and you're going to grade one."

A feeling of coldness came over Cathy and she started shaking. Tears sprung up in her eyes and she felt like she was going to faint. She thought that whole living with Mrs. Wrenn thing was done. She thought going to school in Ontario was done. She thought living with her mother was over.

"You don't think I'm leaving you here again do you? This is a visit Cathy, you are not staying here," Rita said as she stood up and tried to take the dress out of Cathy's hands.

Cathy held on to the dress and she looked her mother directly in the eyes. With a shaky voice she said, "I am not going with you. I am never going with you again. I am staying here." She felt all the blood go out of her face, but she couldn't move; she stood her ground.

"I am your mother and you will do as I say. Now put that dress in the suitcase!" Rita yelled as she pulled the dress out of Cathy's hands.

"That's enough, Rita." Papa had come in the room. He looked at Rita and then he looked at Cathy. He took Cathy's hand and pulled her to him.

"Let her stay."

"No, Daddy, I can't! She's my daughter, I'm taking care of her now and she has to go back with me. This was only a visit!"

"Rita, I am proud that you tried to have Cathy with you, but after hearing the stories from your mother of this Mrs. Wrenn, I don't think it's a good idea for Cathy to live there with you. Cathy has always been perfectly happy here with your mama and me, and I think this is where she should stay."

Rita knew that once her father made up his mind, there was no talking him out of it.

"Well, what do you mean exactly? How long should she stay?"

"She can go to grade one here at home, and maybe next summer when you come back, she can go with you then."

Cathy's heart swelled. She knew Papa would come to her rescue. She turned and buried her face into his rough shirt. Papa put his arms around her and held her close. She heard her mother starting to cry and blowing her nose, but she didn't care, she just wanted to stay in her papa's arms forever.

Rita and Doug left that afternoon. Everyone went to the station to send them off. Rita hugged Cathy and said, "Goodbye, Cathy-o. I'm not mad at you, Hun, I'm just so sad and I am going to miss you like you wouldn't believe. It will be lonesome at Mrs. Wrenn's without you."

Thinking about that wretched Mrs. Wrenn, Cathy started to feel sorry for her mom. Who would wait for her mom to get home from the Laundry? Who would take care of her sore feet? Who would eat the leftover tea and toast her mom left every morning? She started to doubt letting her mother go all by herself, and thought maybe she should get on the train after all, but then she looked down to see Marlene and Janey standing beside her. Marlene was pulling on Cathy's dress and Janey was making funny faces at her.

"Cathy...come and pick blueberries with me," Marlene said in her little voice.

"Me too!" said Janey. "Come ON, Cathy!"

Cathy turned to her mother and said, "Mommy, I promise you I will go back to Ontario, but not until next year, OK?"

She hugged her one last time and then she took Marlene and Janey's hands and ran towards the fields in search of the blueberry bushes.

The rest of the summer was filled with sunshine and happiness. The three girls ran around together, played together, and slept together. Big Molly always brought Little Molly down to Woodward Street and spent most of her days with Nana and the kids. She always made sure to include Cathy, Marlene, and Janey in everything she did. She took them to the shore, took them into Glace Bay, and was often at Nana's to tuck them in at night.

Cathy would often hear Aunt Molly and Nana speaking in low voices at night when they thought the kids were asleep. Cathy didn't really understand what they were talking about, but it always involved Rolfe and someone else named Johnny McGillivary. Cathy thought maybe they were talking about Aunt Tussie's husband, but she was sure his name was Jimmy, not Johnny. It was so confusing with all these names, you could never be sure who anyone was talking about.

Sometimes Georgie and Little Johnny Ryan would come up from Aunt Alice's, and all the cousins would play together in the yard. Cathy sometimes thought Georgie acted a little bossy. She was only a few months older than Cathy, but because she was already going to grade two, she acted like she owned the place. Cathy got along much better with Johnny. He was almost five years older than Cathy, but he was very kind and gentle and always played nice with his little cousins.

Summer turned to fall and fall turned to winter. Aunt Joanie and Uncle Stan got married up in Ontario on October 19, and Cathy was sad that she missed the wedding. She loved Uncle Stan so much and thought her Aunt Joanie was lucky to have such a handsome prince for a husband.

That winter was cold. The little house on Woodward Street was drafty, and the windows rattled when the wind came howling off the ocean. The snow would drift and pile so high sometimes it would block the windows. The wood stove burned day and night trying to keep the place warm. Often the pots and buckets Nana kept full of water would freeze in the night and Papa would have to crack the ice in the morning.

The girls curled up together in the bed, and Nana would lay greatcoats that they kept from the war over top of them. They were heavy and smelled musty, but those old coats kept them warm all night. In the morning, Nana would tell them to get behind the stove to put their clothes on, and she would let them sit in front of the stove on the floor to have their breakfast before Cathy would head to school.

Marlene and Janey were still too young for school. Cathy thought they were so lucky to be able to stay home with Nana all day long, but she liked her teachers and the other kids and Aunt Rosie would often walk Cathy down to St. John's school. Once she was there, Cathy would find Georgie and they would play together at recess. Aunt Rosie would come to pick her up again to take her back home. Sometimes Aunt Rosie would be talkative and sometimes she wouldn't say a word. You never really knew with Aunt Rosie. One minute she'd be singing old

Irish songs and laughing and telling jokes, and the next minute her eyes would turn dark and she'd look at you like she wanted to kill you. Aunt Tussie told Cathy that when Aunt Rosie was little, she got kicked in the head by a horse, but Cathy didn't know for sure.

Every once in a while, Nana would get a letter from Rita with a five-dollar bill in it to help with the groceries, and there would always be a separate note for Cathy. Her mom would tell her all about what Kenny and Susan were up to and how Christmas was sad without Cathy. In the letter, she included a photo of Susan Wrenn sitting in a chair in front of the Christmas tree with a new little doll she got for Christmas. She wrote about how Uncle Doug and Aunt Elsie got a new dog named Barney and how Uncle Stan and Aunt Joanie moved into a house on Rebecca Street. She said that she was hoping that Aunt Joanie might have a baby by next year. She talked about the Laundry, about how Walter would take her dancing and how she would visit and play cards with her friend Ella Jackson.

She talked about going to Brantford to visit Aunt Kay and Uncle Frank and that Aunt Kay was going to have a baby soon too. When she would get these letters, Cathy would miss her family in Ontario: the parties, the get-togethers, and her little friends at St. Joseph's Catholic School, especially Ann. She would miss her mom and how they used to sit at the table and drink tea together, and Cathy would listen to the stories her mom would tell about the Barrons in Ingonish and the fun she had with her cousins when she was a little girl. Cathy loved to hear the stories about Nana's brothers and sisters and her mom had such a great memory and a wonderful way of telling stories. She was starting to look forward to next summer when her mother would come for her yearly visit.

With the melting of the snow and ice, spring came in all its glory. The girls didn't need the greatcoats on their bed anymore, and they could go outside without boots for the first time in months. The dead old grass was growing, and the little green shoots that would soon become daffodils and tulips were starting to sprout out of the ground. The chickens tentatively came out of their coop to peck and see what could be found in the newly uncovered earth.

The crazy rooster was strutting around trying to get their attention, but the chickens were more concerned with clucking and pecking and gossiping to each other about what happened in the coop over the winter.

The girls ran through the fields, down to the shore, up the road, and down the tracks. They laughed and played and welcomed the sunshine. May came fast and before they knew it, it was time for all the grade one children to take their First Communion.

Cathy's First Communion

CHAPTER THIRTEEN

Cape Breton-Spring 1957

It was an early May morning, and the window above Cathy's bed was open. She could feel a beautiful, soft spring breeze blowing gently over her face and she knew the soft cotton curtains were billowing out over her head. She smiled and kept her eyes closed; she could smell the salt and the sea and she could hear the seagulls in the distance. She could feel the warm sun on her face and she knew there wouldn't be a cloud in the sky. Today's weather would be perfect because today was her special day.

Last night, just before going to bed, she looked in the compact mirror Nana had given her years before. Cathy had to laugh right out loud because her friend couldn't seem to stop grinning. Cathy grinned back at the little girl; she knew that both of them felt over the moon about all the plans for her big day.

Nana had been preparing for days for her First Communion. The little house on Woodward Street was clean as a whistle: the light blue table cloth was ironed, the chairs were all set up along the wall, and the little porcelain tea set was out with the tiny silver spoons laid all in a row beside it.

But best of all, Cathy could visualize her beautiful dress hanging in the wardrobe. It was white with short puffy sleeves and fell to just above her knees. Nana got her little dainty gloves to wear. She also had a sweet little cap and veil for her head and brand new white ankle socks. The best part of the outfit was the shiny, patent leather high heeled shoes. To Cathy they looked like shoes that could have belonged to Cinderella, if Cinderella had worn leather and not glass.

The day was going to be wonderful! Everyone was going to be there: Nana, Papa, Aunt Molly, Aunt Tussie, Aunt Rosie, and Marlene and Janey of course. Cathy wasn't sure if her Aunt Alice was going to make it because her youngest boy, Frank, was only two and she was busy with him, Georgie, and Little Johnny. Aunt Alice always seemed busy. Whenever Cathy would go to visit her, she was either baking bread or cake in her wood stove or washing her family's clothes in the tub. Aunt Alice always said that her husband would never—not one time—go down into that mine with store bought bread or cake. She was very proud of that fact.

Like Nana, Aunt Alice and Uncle John didn't have hot water or plumbing, so it made doing chores difficult and it took a lot of time.

Cathy knew her aunt worked hard to make sure her kids were clean, well dressed, and living a life without strife. Aunt Alice always said that no matter what happened between her and her husband, or how much they struggled with money, she would make sure her kids were brought up right.

Aunt Tussie probably wouldn't be able to come to her First Communion either because she was also busy with her family down in what they referred to as the Row. Her husband, Jimmy McGillivray, kept her busy cooking and cleaning, and when she wasn't doing that, she was at the church doing the readings and helping the other ladies with the tea and sandwiches they served in the basement.

Cathy loved her Aunt Tussie so much. She was a quiet, calm person who reminded her of Nana. Aunt Tussie always told her stories about when Cathy was a baby and how Aunt Tussie would play with her. For some reason there was a roll of black rubber tread in the corner of the kitchen and Aunt Tussie would roll it across the floor towards Cathy. She called it "The Schooby" and it scared the living daylights out of little Cathy. Aunt Tussie didn't have a mean bone in her body, but she thought Cathy's reaction to The Schooby was hilarious! She would roll the tread back up, take Cathy in her arms and give her doughy bread and blue tea to make her feel better.

As the years went by, Aunt Tussie seemed to get more and more nervous, especially if Papa was hollering or if Francis was acting up. She would run out of the house and back to her place in the Row in Bridgeport. Then if Jimmy was drinking or getting out of hand, she would run back up to Nana's house. Poor Aunt Tussie, the only place she really seemed comfortable was at either St. John's church, Immaculate Conception, or St. Eugene's or wherever they needed her.

By this time, in 1957, the house was emptying out. Rita, Aunt Kay and Uncle Doug and Uncle Mickey and Aunt Joanie were all up in Ontario. So now it was just Nana and Papa, Aunt Rosie (who was sixteen now), Marlene, Janey and, of course, that stupid article, Francis.

Papa was having a hard time controlling Francis these days. They both worked in the mine now, but Francis was making trouble with the other men and was drinking his money away before giving it to Nana, like he was supposed to. He often came home drunk and would start a fight with Papa. He would go on about how Papa always favoured Dougie, like Dougie could do no wrong. Francis would remind his father that Dougie left for Ontario and married that woman from the West Indies, and just because he came back every summer to visit the family, didn't mean he was the man of the house second in line to Papa. As far as Francis was concerned, Doug was a visitor and he shouldn't be getting any special attention.

He, Francis explained over and over, was the one who stayed, took care of Papa and Mama and went to work every day. *He* was the poor bugger in the mines all day long, week in, and week out. He deserved some respect from his parents, but all he ever got was the two of them going on about him having a few drinks once in a while.

There was nothing worse, in Cathy's opinion, than when Francis was drinking. She shuddered with the thought of him crashing his way into the house, demanding that Nana take care of him, wash his filthy clothes, and make him supper.

"Come on my dear, it's time to wake up and get you ready," Nana said gently as she sat on the bed beside Cathy.

"Morning, Nana," Cathy said as uncomfortable thoughts of Francis vanished. "I can't wait to get that dress on. I'm going to feel like Cinderella!" Cathy sat up and kissed Nana on the cheek.

She knew Nana had been planning this day for a long time and she felt proud to have so much attention from her grandmother. Lord knows Nana was busy enough with Marlene and Janey and all the new grandbabies that were coming one after another, and Cathy knew that her First Communion celebration was something that Nana thought was extra special. After the mass and the communion and the photos with the Bishop, the family went back to Woodward Street to have their lunch. Over tea and cake, Papa commented on how beautiful little Cathy was in her dress and veil and how proud he was of her.

Cathy wished that her mother could have been there to see her, and so she decided she would write her a letter and tell her all about her day. But first, she would change into her play clothes and help Marlene and Janey get into theirs.

As the three girls ran out to check on the kittens in the shed, the rooster watched from his perch and the chickens discussed what should be done about that strutting rooster.

Stan's father and sister, Stan, Joanie, and Doug

CHAPTER FOURTEEN

Cape Breton-Fall 1957

Cathy's mother came back to Cape Breton in July of 1957 to spend two weeks with her family and to collect her daughter. After so long, Cathy was after getting to miss her mother, and she was looking forward to seeing her.

Rita came off the train, once again with her hair done, her red lipstick on, and a nice new summer dress. She looked slim, refreshed and vibrant. She was laughing and joking and telling them all about life in Ontario and about how happy she was.

Cathy wondered if maybe she had found her own apartment and had moved their things out of Mrs. Wrenn's. Wouldn't that be grand, their own apartment with their own kitchen and bathroom? Anything would have been better than that dingy old room in Mrs. Wrenn's house—anything.

But no, her mother had not moved. She said she didn't make very much money at the Laundry, and with her sending money back home every month, rent, and everything else, she couldn't afford her own place. She talked about "poor Kenny and Susan", and how much they missed Cathy, and how they had no one to watch TV with or play with after school. Cathy didn't really care a fig about how much they missed her—she certainly didn't miss them. Well, maybe that wasn't totally true. Susan was a nice little girl, but she was three years younger than Cathy and acted too much like a baby.

This time around, at the end of the two weeks, when Rita came into the room to pack Cathy's things, Cathy didn't put up a fuss. She helped her mother, and when Marlene and Janey came in the room, she let them help her too. How could she go back to Ontario and leave those two little buggers? She loved them so much; they were like sisters to her.

"You two take care of those kittens and the dog," Cathy said as she hugged them goodbye. "Don't get hit by a train when you play on the tracks, and don't go down to the shore by yourselves because you'll get swept away by a wave. Oh, and don't stand too close to the cliffs because the ground is soft and you'll fall right into the ocean."

Cathy worried about them because no one would take as good a care as she did. Nana was too busy baking, cleaning, and washing to keep her eye on them all the time, and that Marlene sure liked to take off on her own. Sometimes Cathy would run around for hours looking for her and then she'd find her sitting in the field, or down the road, or off chasing cats somewhere.

She hugged Aunt Tussie, Big Molly, Little Molly, and Aunt Rosie, and then she ran to Nana and held on to her for what seemed like hours. Nana looked at her with her big brown eyes and said, "Cathy, I always thought you were the calm, cool, and collected one, and I know you'll be alright." She gave her a two dollar bill and a Kleenex full of mints. "You go on dear, you go on with your Ma."

Cathy didn't feel calm, cool, and collected, but she decided at that moment that she wouldn't let Nana down and she would try her best to be the girl that Nana thought she was. Cathy wiped away the tears that were streaming down her cheeks and tried to look as calm as possible.

Papa had already said goodbye to her earlier that morning. He had to go to work, so he gently woke her up when it was still dark and took her in his arms. He hugged her tightly and kissed her on the top of her head.

"You're a good girl, Cathy. You're smart and you're kind and you're a strong girl and you'll be fine," he said as a tear fell silently down his cheek. He took out his handkerchief and blew his nose. He smiled, patted her on the head, and left the room.

They were back on the train and pulling into the Stratford station two days later. This time there was someone waiting for them at the station; it was Walter "Glass Whiskey".

"Heya, Rita! Hey there, Cathy," Walter said as he took their cases and put them in his trunk. He took Rita into his arms and gave her a big kiss on the lips. Rita laughed and pushed him away. As he opened the door for Cathy, he ruffled her hair. She got in quickly and tried to fix her hairdo; she didn't like when he did that.

"Gotta drop you off at the Wrenn's right away, Rita; no time for lunch like I was hoping. Got called into work."

"That's OK, Walter. Why don't you drop us off at the river and then Cathy and I can have a nice walk back to Brant Street. You can bring our cases to Mrs. Wrenn's if you don't mind."

Cathy had forgotten how much she loved the Avon River. She didn't know much about William Shakespeare or about his plays, but Stratford was becoming famous because of the theatre. People were coming from all over the place to see the Stratford Shakespearean Festival. They had just built a new beautiful building where they held the festival and Cathy was still hoping that her mother would take her there one day.

Down by the river, the beautiful white swans were swimming around and once in a while they would come up on the grass and eat bread that the children would feed them. Cathy was too afraid to feed the swans, she saw one of them bite a little boy once, so she stayed back and admired them from a safe distance.

"Let's walk towards the old pump house," Rita said as she took Cathy's hand. "I was so lonesome without you, Cathy. Did you miss me too?"

"Yes, Mommy, I missed you. I missed Doug and Elsie too, and I was so sad to miss Joanie and Stan's wedding. Was it beautiful?"

"Oh, yes! Your Aunt Joanie looked like a princess and Uncle Stan was as charming and handsome as ever. But you know what? Susan and Kenny really missed you, Hun. I bet you can't wait to see them."

"Let's keep walking, Mommy. I don't want to go back yet."

They walked through the pine trees near the old pump house and took the long way back around the park before they headed to 28 Brant Street.

As they walked towards the house, Cathy felt as if the sun went behind a cloud. Suddenly it seemed dark and she felt like it was getting hard to breath. She stopped walking and took her mom's hand.

"What's wrong, Cathy?" Rita looked worried. The colour had drained out of Cathy's face and she was white as a sheet.

"I can't," was all she could manage to say. She didn't know what was wrong with her, she couldn't move her feet. Suddenly, a wave of anxiety washed over her as she remembered her life at Mrs. Wrenn's: the bird, the *Beacon*, the cereal, the underpants.

"I can't," she said again.

Her mother looked like she didn't know what to do. She had stopped and looked to see if someone could help her, but no one was around.

"Hun, you're alright," she said. "Maybe you just need something to eat. Come on in and I'll fix you a sandwich."

Cathy let her lead her to the house, in the door, and up the stairs. Luckily it seemed like no one else was home. Cathy sat at the table and started to feel better, but she knew now that she hated this place. She wasn't sure when it happened exactly, but she hated it and she wasn't sure if she could stand living here again.

The next day her mother went to work as usual. Cathy could hardly believe that she had just spent the last year and a half at Nana's and now, suddenly, she was here again in this hateful house. Maybe it would be better now? Maybe Mrs. Wrenn would be nicer. Maybe Susan would be more like a big girl and they could actually play.

Just before she got herself ready for the day, she looked in the mirror to check on her friend.

"How are you doing this morning?" she asked. "How do you feel about being back here?"

The little girl raised her eyebrows and shrugged her shoulders as if to say that she didn't really feel any different about the situation.

"You know what? I think things might be a bit better now," Cathy told the little girl, trying to act more positive. "Maybe Mrs. Wrenn had some peace and quiet while I was away and maybe she felt bad about how mean she's been to us. Let's get dressed and go down to the kitchen and see what's what."

The little girl appeared doubtful, but she straightened her shoulders and took a deep breath and moved away from the mirror. Cathy got dressed and went down to the kitchen.

"Well, look what the cat dragged in," was the first thing Mrs. Wrenn said to her after a year and a half. Cathy secretly cringed when she heard that British accent.

Cathy smiled weakly and sat down. "Hello, Mrs. Wrenn. Hi, Kenny. Hi, Susan."

Kenny stuck his tongue out at her, but Susan gave her a big smile.

"We missed you, Cathy! Me and my dolly. See? I got a new one for Christmas."

"That's a nice dolly, Susan. What's her name?" Cathy asked.

"Eat your cereal, Cathy. You can talk when you're done," Mrs. Wrenn ordered.

That shut Cathy up. For God's sake, could she not even say hello to the kids?

After school Cathy came home, and instead of going in the house, she sat on the front porch. It was September and the weather was warm and the sun was hours away from setting. She went through her lunch bag and found a leftover apple. While she sat eating it, she thought about her new class and her new teacher. She recognized a few children from her kindergarten class, and the teacher seemed to remember her too, even though Cathy wasn't at the school for grade one.

Up and down the street kids were coming home from school. They would go in their houses, drop their bags off, get a snack, and head outdoors again.

Kenny came walking up the street with a boy and a girl that Cathy hadn't seen before.

"Hey, Cathy!" Kenny greeted her as he got closer to the house. "These are my new friends, Georgie English and Elaine Soeder. Elaine lives down the street, and Georgie moved in next door last year."

Cathy thought it was funny that this little boy had the same name as her cousin down home.

"Hi. Nice to meet you." Cathy stood up.

"Nice to meet you too," said Elaine.

They were a little shy of each other at first, but then the boys started playing kick the can and the girls soon joined in. More kids came out to play and soon the street was full of children playing, adults out walking, and dogs and cats roaming the streets. It was still warm as the sun was setting over the horizon, the crickets were chirping, and the cicadas were letting everyone know that summer was over. Soon the wind would change and the smell of dried and dying leaves would fill the air. The sun would set earlier and the air would turn chill. But for now, everyone enjoyed the end of summer and as night fell, they all went back in their houses to rest and relax with their families.

Mrs. Wrenn called the children for supper. They took their places, and after playing outside for so long, they were thirsty. Cathy reached for her glass of milk and just before she could drink it, Mrs. Wrenn said, "Not until you're done your supper."

Cathy had forgotten that rule. She had to finish her supper before she was allowed to have a drink. She remembered how Aunt Elsie would give her a drink and tell her to "wash it down." She liked to have a drink with her meal, not after.

Reluctantly, Cathy put the glass back down and started to eat. In the meantime, both Kenny and Susan drank down their glasses of cold milk. Cathy was going to say something, but she looked at Mrs. Wrenn and the look on her face was as if to say, *My children can drink milk when they want to, but not you, Cathy;*

you have to wait. Cathy's face got hot and she wanted to throw the milk in Mrs. Wrenn's face, but instead she quietly ate her watery, tasteless supper of cabbage, boiled potatoes, and meatloaf.

After supper, Mrs. Wrenn told Cathy that she had to clear the table. She was old enough now to do some work around the house and clearing the table would be a good start. Cathy noticed that Kenny and Susan jumped up and ran into the TV room. She started to say something to Mrs. Wrenn, but she had already turned to the sink and started to do the dishes, as if she didn't notice. Cathy sighed and started clearing the table, hoping that her mother would be home soon.

It was dark and Kenny and Susan had already gone to bed. Mrs. Wrenn sent Cathy upstairs because she didn't like her to be in the living room when Mr. and Mrs. Wrenn sat to watch the news. Cathy made a tea and sat at the table to wait for her mom. Rita still wasn't home by the time she finished her tea, so she got her nighty on and wondered where the heck her mother was. She went downstairs to brush her teeth and go to the bathroom and figured her mom would be upstairs when she went back up. But she still wasn't home, so Cathy got under the blankets and lay there with the lights on. She must have fallen asleep because all of a sudden she heard her mother coughing and she could smell cigarette smoke. Cathy sat up and hit her head on the stupid ceiling.

"Mom! Where were you?" she said as she rubbed her forehead.

"Hi, Hun. How was your day?" Rita answered from the table.

"No! I said, where were you?" Cathy was getting upset.

Did her mother forget that she lived here again?

"Oh, I met Walter uptown and he wanted to take me to supper. Didn't you have your supper with the Wrenns?" Her words sounded slurred and her eyes were red.

"Walter? Mom, I just got here, you should have come home right away. I was waiting for you."

"I'm sorry, Cathy-o," she said as she tapped her cigarette into the filthy ashtray. "Walter is such a sweetheart. You know we're really in love, Cathy? You should see how nice he treats me."

She tilted her head to the side and squinted at Cathy through the smoke. Cathy suddenly felt so frustrated she didn't know what to say. She just wanted to yell something at her mom. Something that would explain how she was feeling.

"Go to sleep now Hun, it's late."

Cathy turned over and pulled the blanket over her head.

She was shaking with anger.

The next morning when she woke up, her mother was already gone. Cathy was tired and instantly in a bad mood when she remembered her mother being out so late last night.

She got dressed and went over to the table and found her usual crust of toast and half a cup of tea. She slumped in her chair and ate the toast. At least there was still a bit of marmalade on it.

She started to feel bad that she was so angry with her mother. She knew how hard Rita worked at the Laundry and she also knew how much she liked Walter. They had been dating for at least three years. You'd think he would have married her by now. Cathy wondered why he hadn't asked her yet. Kay and Frank, Joanie and Stan, Mickey and Alma, and Doug and Elsie were all married. All the aunts down home were married, except for Rosie, so it did seem kind of odd that her mother was still single. She was 34 already, no spring chicken.

Cathy suddenly felt sorry for her mom. It must be hard to be a single woman trying to take care of her daughter all by herself. The only money she had was what she brought home from the Laundry, and sending half of it back home didn't leave much left over—Cathy knew it was hard trying to make ends meet.

She guessed her mom's life would be happier if she had a man that loved her. Cathy didn't know how she felt about Walter, but it would sure be nice if he would marry her mother. Then maybe they could all live in a house and have supper together and be a happy family.

Debbie and Cathy in Goderich

CHAPTER FIFTEEN

Stratford-Spring/Summer 1958

Several long months had passed and nothing in the Wrenn household had changed. It was morning once again and Cathy's mom had already gone to work. Cathy was still lying in bed dreading the thought of going down to the kitchen when she heard Mrs. Wrenn at the bottom of the stairs.

"Cathy! Come down the stairs this instant!"

Oh, God! What did she want? Cathy slowly got out of the bed and went and stood at the top of the stairs.

"Lift up your nighty! I want to see if you're behaving yourself."

Cathy froze. What? Lift up her nighty? She wasn't going to lift up her nighty. Mrs. Wrenn huffed and started making her way up the stairs; Cathy backed away towards Kenny's bed.

"Lift it up, now!" Mrs. Wrenn said.

Cathy slowly pulled up her nighty and saw the look of anger pass over Mrs. Wrenn's face. "You little devil, you're wearing your underpants! How many times have I told you to take them off at night?" She started shaking with anger, and Cathy put her hands up in case she was going to hit her. "This is your last chance, young Miss. I am going to come up these stairs every morning from now on to make sure you're behaving, and if I find you with underpants on again, you and your mother will be kicked out of this house for good!" She spun on her heel and stomped back down the stairs.

Cathy let her nighty fall down to her knees. She couldn't move; she was frozen. After a few moments, she walked slowly over to the mirror. She didn't have to stand on her tippy toes anymore. She was tall enough to see her friend, and her friend's face was drained of all colour; her eyes were as big as saucers and she looked frightened.

Cathy suddenly realized why her mother didn't say anything to Mrs. Wrenn, why she didn't stick up for her daughter, and why they didn't move out. Rita was afraid of Mrs. Wrenn. She was afraid of what Mrs. Wrenn would say or what she would do. There were times when it seemed like her mother got along all right with Mrs. Wrenn, but even during those rare moments, her mother always seemed wary of the woman, as if she didn't trust her. Cathy wondered if something had happened to her mother in the past, if at some time in her life she felt helpless and unable to defend herself. But Cathy knew one thing, if her mother was truly afraid of Mrs. Wrenn, then Cathy was too.

Then new feelings bubbled up, ones she had never felt before. Besides feeling afraid, she also felt embarrassed, she felt let down. She realized her mother was weak and couldn't or wouldn't defend herself or her daughter. What kind of a mother is so afraid of someone that she would allow her daughter to go through life like this? If her mother wasn't going to stick up for her, who would? She felt ashamed of herself and of her mother.

She would never tell her aunts and uncles about the way Mrs. Wrenn treated her. For the life of her, she couldn't figure out why Mrs. Wrenn was so mean. Did she hate kids? Did she even like her own children? Why would she adopt Kenny and Susan if she didn't want them? It would forever be a mystery to her.

The little girl in the mirror's face was stony, and her eyes seemed empty. No tears, no emotion, just a stillness that frightened Cathy. She moved away from the mirror, got back into bed, and closed her eyes.

Spring had sprung and Cathy turned 8 years old on April 18. She had her party at Uncle Doug and Aunt Elsie's just like before. For Easter, her mother bought her a new blue blazer. All the girls in school were wearing them. Hers had shiny brass buttons and an emblem sewn on the left breast pocket. She thought she looked really cute with her white dress and her white hat that she wore to church, and best of all, the black patent leather dress shoes with the straps across the ankles. Susan also had a blazer and hat and even the same little Easter purse. Rita thought it would be cute if they looked like twins. Cathy was almost four years older than Susan, had black hair and Susan had blond hair, but she guessed maybe they did sort of look alike. She wondered if anyone thought they were sisters.

Cathy loved school, and now that the weather was warmer, she enjoyed her walks back and forth to St. Joseph's. She had a few friends that she was close with, especially Myra Hall. She was a small, slim girl with beautiful blond hair that was almost white. She looked like a little angel. They played at recess and ate lunch together under a big tree in the school yard. She wished she could play with Myra after school too, but she would never in a million years invite her to where she lived.

After school, she would walk slowly back to 28 Brant Street, knowing that she would be forced to play with Kenny. She would much rather play with Elaine, but whenever Georgie wasn't available, Mrs. Wrenn would make her play with Kenny. She had to play whatever he wanted. If she didn't play the way he wanted her to, he would have a temper tantrum and throw toys at her. Mrs. Wrenn would come rushing in the room to see what the commotion was and then of course give Cathy heck, as if she had done something wrong.

After supper, Kenny and Susan would head to the living room while Cathy would have to clear the table and do the dishes. Now that she was 8 years old, Mrs. Wrenn said she was old enough to start doing some cleaning as well as clearing the table. She gave her a cloth with coal oil and Cathy would have to get on her hands and knees to clean all the baseboards in the kitchen. Then she would have to take the dust cloth and dust the living room. Kenny and Susan didn't have to do anything. They would just complain that she was in the way of the TV. Cathy was relieved when Kenny and Susan finally had to go to bed because then Mrs. Wrenn would make her go upstairs too.

Her mother used to come home right after work, but for the past several months, she would come home later and later. Cathy knew she was with Walter, but it made her sad that her mother wouldn't come home right after work so they could at least have supper together. The times that Rita would come home early, she would be too busy cutting the corns and calluses off her feet or washing her hair to pay much attention to Cathy.

The apartment would fill with cigarette smoke and she would talk and talk about the women in the Laundry, or Walter, or her friends, but she rarely asked Cathy how she was. It was as if she were afraid of what the answer might be. Cathy thought it was easier for her mother to believe that everything was all right. It was like she was living in a fantasy world, where everyone was happy and no one was sad. Cathy wondered if she had always been that way?

Sometimes when Mrs. Wrenn would send Cathy upstairs, she would follow her up to the room. Cathy would stiffen and get nervous when she heard Mrs. Wrenn behind her. She would walk around the room looking at their things with distaste. She would inspect to make sure that no one had been sitting on Kenny's sacred bed, and if Cathy or Rita had left something on it, she would take it and throw it down on the floor. Then she would run her hand along the dresser and look at the dust on her fingers. She would peer into her mother's bowl of holy water and roll her eyes, and then she would look at the overflowing ashtray and click her tongue with disgust.

Cathy's mother was always neat and tidy about her person, but she was never a good housekeeper. One time, Cathy took the ashtray down to the kitchen to empty the ashes. She ran the ashtray under hot water and was amazed as she watched all the ash residue rinse away and leave a clean glass bottom. She had never seen the bottom of the ashtray before.

Cathy hated how dirty their apartment was, but she hated it even more when Mrs. Wrenn made it seem like they weren't clean. Worse, she would look at Cathy, and while chewing on her humbug say, "That mother of yours, late again. She should be home taking care of her kid, but no, she's out at that hotel again with God only knows who." This made Cathy hate Mrs. Wrenn even more. How dare she speak about her mother like that? Her mother didn't go to hotels. She was just having a nice dinner with her boyfriend and hoping every day he might ask her to marry him. Cathy thought that any day now, her mom would come rushing up the stairs to show Cathy her engagement ring.

After Mrs. Wrenn would finally go downstairs, Cathy would get ready for bed and lie there waiting for her mother to come home. She would fall into a light, agitated sleep and then when she heard her mom cough or sneeze, she knew she was home, and she would finally relax and fall into a deeper sleep.

As soon as her mom would wake up in the morning and leave, Cathy would jump out of bed, quickly take her underpants off and hide them in the drawer and quietly get back under the covers. After a little while, Mrs. Wrenn would creep up the stairs and over to the bed. She would snatch the corner of the blanket and whip it off to see if Cathy was wearing her underpants. When she saw that she was not, she would accuse Cathy of trying to trick her. Disappointed, she would stomp back down the stairs to get breakfast for Kenny and Susan.

Cathy grew to despise the mornings and she would wake up in a cold sweat, worried she slept through her only chance to quickly get her underpants off before Mrs. Wrenn would come and catch her. It used to be that the mornings were her only sanctuary away from the abuse that Mrs. Wrenn constantly directed at her. She used to be able to get up, drink her mother's leftover tea, and eat the leftover toast, but now that Mrs. Wrenn came up every morning to inspect her, the one peaceful moment of the day was spoiled. Cathy's nerves were shot. She didn't sleep well, she always felt tired, she was anxious, and was starting to have a hard time in school.

The only thing that kept her from breaking down completely was the thought that they would be going to Cape Breton as soon as school was over. She would beg Nana and Papa to let her stay. Her plan was to stay for the whole summer, and the following school year, and never go back to Ontario again.

But that was not to be. Near the end of June, Cathy's mother announced that this year, they would not be going to Cape Breton. The train tickets were too expensive and Mrs. Wrenn had decided that when Rita would leave during the summer, she would continue to charge her rent. Just because Rita wanted to go gallivanting off to the East Coast every summer didn't mean that Mrs. Wrenn should suffer the loss of income.

So her mom said that she had decided to make the most of it. She and Cathy would stay in Stratford, take in the theatre, have picnics down by the river, and go window shopping uptown to all the new little stores that were popping up everywhere. The town was growing and getting busier in the summer months with all of the tourists coming to see the festival. It made life a little more hectic; the restaurants were always busy and the prices were increased, but if you were a resident, and the restaurant owners recognized you, they'd give you a "special" menu with the normal prices listed.

Cathy was beside herself. She couldn't get over that she wouldn't be going down home for the summer. She panicked because her plan was to stay there for the next school year and be away from Mrs. Wrenn once and for all. She begged her mother to let her go. She said she could even take the train by herself so her mother could save the price of one ticket.

"That's ridiculous, Cathy. You're only eight years old. You can't go by yourself!"

"Yes, I can, Mom. I walk back and forth to school by myself, I make my own food, I get myself ready every morning and every night. No one helps me do anything, so why shouldn't I be able to take the train alone?"

Rita turned away quickly to the table and her pack of cigarettes. She lit one and looked out the dusty window of the shabby apartment. She didn't say a word. Nothing made Cathy madder. Why didn't her mom say something?? Why did she ignore her every time she brought up something that she didn't like? Cathy wanted to run across the room and take her by the shoulders and shake her to see if she would do something. But Cathy would never do that, not in a million years, so she went and sat on the bed and grabbed the pillow instead. She squished it as hard as she could and then threw it on the floor. That night Rita went out with Walter and didn't come back until well after midnight.

Cathy resigned herself to accept the fact that she wasn't going to Cape Breton. Her mom promised her over and over again that she would let her go next summer, so Cathy decided to make the most of it too. Her mom met a lady named Mrs. Allen. She and her husband had a cottage on Lake Huron outside a town called Goderich. Rita and Cathy were invited to spend two weeks there and Mrs. Allen said there was a little girl that lived nearby that Cathy could play with.

Once they arrived and unpacked their things, Mrs. Allen told them to come outside for lunch. She had a picnic table with a nice white table cloth on it, a vase of fresh cut flowers, and all the plates and utensils were set as if they were expecting the Queen. Mrs. Allen had flowers all over the property and chairs lined up all in a row near the cliff that overlooked the lake. She said she lined them up this way so they could have the best view of the sunset.

"Sunsets in Goderich are famous, and that's why Goderich is known as one of the prettiest towns in Canada," she said proudly. Cathy couldn't wait for the evening so she could see how beautiful the famous sunset would be.

After lunch, a little girl came walking across the lawn. She looked to be about the same age as Cathy and what was funny is that they both had the same hair cut! They had bangs cut straight across the front, and short in the back. Cathy wished her mom would let her hair grow long, but Mrs. Wrenn insisted it was cleaner to have shorter hair.

"Cathy, this is the little girl I was telling you about," Mrs. Allen said as she stood up from the table. "Her name is Debbie. Hello my dear, how are you today?" she greeted the girl.

"Hi, Mrs. Allen! My mom said I could come over for the afternoon, but I have to be home for supper," Debbie said as she looked shyly at Cathy.

"That's fine, dear. Now, this is Cathy. She's from Stratford and she's going to be staying with us for a few weeks. Would you like to play with her?" Mrs. Allen smiled as she sat back down and picked up her teacup.

"Yes!" Debbie answered Mrs. Allen. "Would you like to play, Cathy? I can show you the birdbath."

"OK," Cathy said, starting to smile. Normally she was shy, but this girl seemed so nice Cathy felt comfortable right away.

"Let's go!"

Cathy followed Debbie across the lawn, past the chairs, and over to the birdbath.

The girls grew inseparable and spent the next two weeks like two peas in a pod. They fed the birds and watched them swim around their birdbath. They went to the beach every day and played in the sand and chased the seagulls. They didn't swim much because Cathy didn't know how and Rita was deathly afraid she would drown, so they spent their time running up and down the shore looking for shells and driftwood.

Every night when the sky was clear, Cathy, Debbie, Rita, and Mr. and Mrs. Allen would make themselves comfortable in the chairs and get ready to watch the beautiful ball of fire sink towards the horizon and down into the great lake. They would clap their hands and sing funny songs like "Day is done, gone the sun." The girls would jump up and salute the setting sun and look forward to the next day when they could enjoy its warmth again.

Cathy would never forget that summer. It wasn't the Atlantic Ocean and it wasn't Marlene and Janey, but Lake Huron and her friend Debbie created memories that, for Cathy, would last forever.

Stan, baby Theresa, Rita, Cathy, Doug and friend

CHAPTER SIXTEEN

Stratford-Fall 1958

It was raining after school and none of the kids were outside playing, so Kenny, Susan, and Cathy went to the living room as usual and watched TV. The kids were into *The Little Rascals* now and they were all sitting on the floor laughing at Alfalfa, Buckwheat and Darla, but they really got a kick out of the dog, Petey.

Kenny turned to look at Cathy and said, "You look like Darla, Cathy."

Cathy felt embarrassed because she secretly thought Darla was really pretty. She was thinking about how she could do her hair like Darla, and subconsciously had her thumb in her mouth, biting at the skin around her nail.

"Get that out of your mouth!" Out of nowhere, Mrs. Wrenn smacked her hand out of her mouth, grabbed her by the arm and pulled her into the kitchen. She held Cathy by her wrists and yelled into her face, "What did I say about that nasty, dirty habit?"

Cathy was stunned. She didn't know what to do. She tried pulling her hands back, but Mrs. Wrenn held them firmly.

"I have a fix for that bad habit." She went to the cupboard and took down the pepper shaker. She grabbed Cathy's hand and shook pepper onto her thumb. "Now stick that in your mouth and see how you like it!"

Cathy looked at her like she was insane.

"No!" was all she could manage to say.

Mrs. Wrenn grabbed her shoulders and pushed her into the chair.

"This will help with your sauciness too." She grabbed Cathy's thumb again and poured more pepper over it. She forced her thumb into Cathy's mouth and held it there.

"You suck on that and then let me know how saucy you want to be!"

Cathy was in shock. She tried to pull her thumb out of her mouth, but Mrs. Wrenn held it fast. She tried to spit out the pepper, but it wouldn't come out. Tears started streaming down her face, the pepper was so awful. Mrs. Wrenn held the back of her head, and her hand, and wouldn't let go. Cathy started screaming but it was all muffled. Mrs. Wrenn blinked her eyes and shook her head, as if coming out of a daze. She let go of Cathy's head and hand.

"Now go over there and get a drink of water, but I swear to you, if I ever catch that thumb in your mouth again, you'll be sorry." She put the pepper back in the cupboard and left the room.

Cathy could hardly drink the water. She wasn't crying and she wasn't screaming. She felt scared to death. What had just happened? She would never get over it. She put the glass in the sink, walked past Kenny and Susan, who were standing in the doorway with their eyes opened wide, and went slowly up the stairs to wait for her mom.

It was useless. No matter what Cathy said to her mom, she wouldn't listen. Cathy told her about the pepper and about the milk and about how Mrs. Wrenn seemed crazy and how she was getting worse. Her mom just busied herself putting laundry away and tidying up the room. Didn't she hear her?

Finally, she turned to Cathy and said, "Cathy, I know that Mrs. Wrenn isn't the nicest lady in the world, but she's letting us live here for real cheap. I've heard about other apartments uptown, but they're all too expensive." She sat at the table. "I think that if you just come home from school and come right up the stairs, you won't get into so much trouble."

"But Mom, she won't let me! She makes me stay downstairs and play with Kenny and Susan. She doesn't like when I'm up here by myself because she thinks I'm going to get up to something."

Cathy didn't know what she could possibly do up here by herself to get into trouble, unless she sat on Kenny's stupid bed. "Can't you say something to her? Can't you tell her to leave me alone?"

"She's not that bad, is she Cathy?" Rita sighed.

Cathy didn't go into all of the details about what happened in the kitchen. She couldn't tell her mom about how Mrs. Wrenn actually held her thumb in her mouth and how she almost gagged from the taste of the pepper. She only said that Mrs. Wrenn put pepper on her thumb and made her put it in her mouth.

"I've heard of mothers washing their children's mouths out with soap, and although I don't think that's very nice, at least the children stop swearing or being saucy or whatever they're doing."

Cathy couldn't believe it. Nana would never do something like that. How could her mother think that was OK? She couldn't stand it any longer. She didn't want to live in the house with her mother anymore. She had to get back to Cape Breton. She had to get back to Nana.

The next morning Mrs. Wrenn came upstairs to tell Cathy to come down for breakfast, and even though she would have rather stayed upstairs and have toast and tea, she thought she'd better get down there before Mrs. Wrenn came back up.

She sat at the table in front of the bowl of Grape-Nuts. She desperately wanted more milk to fill up the bowl, but she didn't bother asking, she knew what the answer would be.

There was a knock at the door and Mrs. Wrenn went and opened it for the bread man. There was nothing better than the bread man. He would come once in a while when the Wrenns would put in an order, with a basket full of freshly baked buns, cakes, and bread. After she paid him and shut the door, Mrs. Wrenn brought the basket, covered with a cloth, into the kitchen and put it on the table. She lifted off the cloth and the mouth-watering smell of baked bread filled the kitchen.

Cathy was sort of in shock because she realized that Mrs. Wrenn must have invited her to breakfast this morning knowing the bread man was coming. Cathy couldn't believe her luck, her stomach growled at the thought of that hot bread smothered in jam.

Mrs. Wrenn handed Kenny and Susan each a plate and with a pair of tongs, gave them each a hot roll. Cathy patiently waited her turn while Mrs. Wrenn took out a third roll, and instead of putting it on Cathy's plate, she put it on her own. Cathy's heart started beating faster and her face got all red. Don't tell me. Please don't tell me she's not going to give me one, Cathy thought. Mrs. Wrenn looked at her, tilted her head to the side and squinted her eyes. "Eat your cereal, Cathy." She smirked, spread a huge dollop of jam on her bun and took a big bite.

After breakfast, Cathy couldn't bring herself to go to school. She went upstairs and peered into the mirror, almost embarrassed to see how the little girl was reacting. Her friend was slowly shaking her head back and forth, her lips were pursed together, her nostrils were flared and her eyes were huge and full of shock. It was as if she wanted to say, I just can't believe this is happening to us.

"I know," whispered Cathy. "I hate that woman and I hate this life." And without any more energy to try to make the girl feel better, she pushed herself roughly away from the mirror and crawled back into bed.

When her mother came home that night, Cathy didn't say a word. She wondered if Mrs. Wrenn told her mother that she didn't go to school. After this morning's episode, she couldn't bring herself to go.

"What's wrong, Hun? Bad day at school?" Rita asked as she changed out of her uniform.

"School was fine, Mom," Cathy said quietly as she sat on the bed holding her doll. Obviously, Mrs. Wrenn didn't notice that Cathy stayed home for the day, and her mom couldn't tell that she just lied about school.

"Well, that's good," Rita said as she took off her nylons and put on her slippers.

"Did I tell you that it's little Theresa's baptism this weekend? We're all going to Immaculate Conception for mass and then we're having a reception at Doug and Elsie's afterwards."

Cathy looked at her doll's face and thought about her new little cousin, Theresa. Aunt Joanie and Uncle Stan were over the moon about her, and so was she. Theresa was born on April 15, 1958, just three days before Cathy's birthday. She had soft blond hair and big brown eyes. When Cathy got to hold her, she would wrap her little hand around Cathy's fingers and hold on tight. Cathy often got to feed her and while she was drinking from her bottle, Theresa would smile her big toothless grin and giggle when Cathy would wipe the milk that dribbled down her chin. Cathy thought Theresa was the cutest thing she ever saw and although she was still upset with her mother, the thought of holding Theresa made her feel a little better.

"C'mon in, girls! Take your coats off and stay awhile!" Aunt Elsie said in her sing-song voice as she took their coats and hung them in the closet.

"Hey there Reet, Cathy. Nice church ceremony, eh?" Uncle Doug said in one short breath.

"Yes Dougie, little Theresa was the belle of the ball," Rita answered as she took off her boots.

Theresa *had* been the belle of the ball at the church. One of Uncle Stan's sisters gave Aunt Joanie a long white gown that had been passed down through the family, and Aunt Elsie had crocheted a beautiful white blanket to wrap Theresa in.

Theresa was as good as gold through the whole ceremony and only made one little noise when the water was poured over her head. She was such a darlin' and Cathy got to hold her while they sat in the pew during mass. Cathy was also excited because Aunt Joanie bought her a new purse that she could have at church. Inside the purse, Aunt Joanie had put some candies and a prayer card for her to look at during the ceremony.

At Doug and Elsie's, everyone took turns holding Theresa. Rita kept saying that she couldn't get over how Theresa kept looking at her, even when she was being held by Uncle Stan. When Theresa needed a diaper change, Aunt Joanie let Cathy help her. Cathy didn't mind putting the cream on her little bum, but she let Aunt Joanie pin the diaper because she would never forgive herself if she pricked Theresa with one of those giant pins. Afterwards, Cathy sat in the rocking chair and held Theresa until she fell asleep. Even though Cathy's arm was falling asleep too, she wouldn't move because she didn't want Theresa to wake up. She looked like a little angel and Cathy wished she could hold her forever.

As she was rocking in the chair and listening to the adults talk, she remembered the story Nana told her about when she was a baby. She would have been older than Theresa, probably two or three years old.

Nana had been doing the laundry and, unlike the washers they had these days, Nana still used a wringer washer. While Cathy stood on a chair, watching the clothes go back and forth in the agitator, Nana would take the soaking wet clothes from the water and feed them through the rollers. When the clothes came out the other side, all of the water would be wrung out of them.

Cathy was curious about how the rollers worked and how the clothes went through. Nana kept telling her to keep her hands away from the wringer, but when Nana went outside to get another pail of water, Cathy noticed that one of Papa's shirts was getting stuck. The machine started making an awful racket and Cathy looked to see if Nana was on her way back in. She could see Nana through the window, filling the pail up over at the well.

The machine was making all kinds of noise trying to get the shirt through, but it was all bunched up in the rollers. Cathy reached over with one hand and got a hold of the wet shirt to see if she could pull it back through. When she pulled, she almost lost her balance, so she leaned over even farther and grabbed the shirt with both hands. She pulled as hard as she could, but the shirt wouldn't come back out.

Then, all of a sudden, the shirt started going through again, and she was losing her balance and was afraid to fall. She held onto the shirt and realized that her hands were heading towards the rollers, but before she could let go, the rollers pulled her right hand all the way through.

She screamed as Nana took hold of her arm and pulled it as hard as she could. Nana got her hand out from between the rollers and swept Cathy into her arms and ran over to the rocking chair. She sat with Cathy held to her chest, holding her sore hand. Cathy cried and cried and Nana rocked and rocked. Nana didn't say a word, but she held Cathy for the rest of the afternoon and left the clothes soaking in the tub. She didn't turn the wringer on again for weeks.

Cathy looked at her hand as she rocked Theresa, and could still see the faint white scar she had across her fingers. She looked down at the baby and thought to herself, "I will never let anything happen to you. You are a precious, precious girl and I will love you your whole life."

Twenty-three years later, her little cousin Theresa would die in a car accident. Cathy's heart would break, and even though Aunt Joanie and Uncle Stan had three other children, Joanie would never be the same again.

Susan Wrenn

CHAPTER SEVENTEEN

Stratford-Winter 1958

Cathy couldn't understand how Mrs. Wrenn could ruin absolutely anything and everything that was good in life. It was Christmas Eve and her mother, unbelievably, was out. She said the Laundry was having a Christmas party and her boss, Lux, insisted that she go. Cathy couldn't believe it! Couldn't her mother have said that her daughter was home alone with the wretched Wrenns? That the most important night of the year was Christmas Eve and it should be spent with family?

Rita gave her a reproachful look. "Hun, I'll only go out for a few hours. There's a dinner and a dance and I promise I'll only stay for the dinner part and then I'll be home." She smiled weakly at Cathy, but Cathy just sat at the kitchen table, clenching her teeth and shaking her head.

She grabbed a pencil and planned to start drawing on a brown paper bag she had, but while her mother was brushing her hair and humming to herself, Cathy started scribbling on the paper. At first she pressed lightly but as each second ticked by and she realized that her mother was ignoring her, she pressed harder and harder until the lines were black and about to tear through the paper.

She felt the tears well up in her eyes, but she swore to God that she wouldn't let them fall. She didn't want her mom to think that she was sad because she wasn't sad, she was furious. She wanted to scream, she wanted to yell, she wanted to throw the pencil at her mother's back, but she just kept scribbling until finally the pencil broke.

"OK Hun, bye for now. We'll see you soon!" Rita gave her a little wave from across the room. She didn't even come over to kiss her. She was probably afraid of being too close to Cathy because she knew Cathy was mad at her. Once she went down the steps, Cathy whipped the pencil at the doorway and with a sob let the tears fall.

After a while Mrs. Wrenn called up and told her to come downstairs for supper. Mr. Wrenn was home and Cathy was glad because whenever he was at the table, Mrs. Wrenn acted like she was a nice person, and even though it made Cathy's stomach turn to see her acting so phoney, it was better than worrying about what Mrs. Wrenn might do if she got angry.

After supper, Mr. Wrenn put some Christmas music on and lit the lights on the tree. They had a puny little tree that wasn't real with tinsel hanging off of it and a few bulbs here and there. Cathy thought it was a sorry excuse for a tree, but at least they actually celebrated Christmas and the lights made the dreary living room look a little festive.

Mrs. Wrenn told the kids to sit at the kitchen table and colour in the new Christmas colouring books they bought at the church bazaar last weekend. Kenny ripped out a sheet from his book for Cathy and rolled some crayons across the table so that she could colour too. The music was nice and Mr. Wrenn offered them some Christmas cookies he'd bought on the way home. Cathy was actually having fun munching away at her cookie and colouring, and her mind drifted to thoughts of what she might get from Santa Claus tomorrow morning.

All week at school they were talking about Santa and his elves and how they were busy at the North Pole making toys for all the good little girls and boys. Cathy knew that she was a good girl and she couldn't help but smile to herself hoping that Santa might bring her a new book to read or maybe her own set of crayons. She imagined all the reindeer getting ready to pull Santa's sleigh across the night sky and how they would land on the roof and make sure Santa got safely down the chimney.

She hoped he realized that she was upstairs in the attic and that he wouldn't forget to leave a gift for her. She knew that instead of leaving gifts under the tree like he did at Nana's, here in Ontario he left them in the children's stockings. She noticed there were only two stockings hanging from the mantle in the living room, but she knew that as soon as her mom got home, she would hang Cathy's stocking from the mantle too.

After a little while, Mrs. Wrenn announced that it was time for bed. Cathy wasn't disappointed because the sooner she went to bed the sooner Santa would arrive. She checked the clock; it was almost eight o'clock and she knew her mom would come through the door at any minute. She waited for Kenny and Susan to pack up their colouring but then Mrs. Wrenn said, "Cathy, I told you, it's time for bed, now get going."

"Aren't Kenny and Susan going too?" she asked.

"Well since you're so nosy, and you have to know everything, no, they are not going to bed yet," Mrs. Wrenn said. "Kenny and Susan, you two go in the living room. There's a Christmas special coming on the TV in a few minutes and you can stay up late to watch it."

Now Cathy was disappointed. Why did she have to go to bed and they got to stay up? God! Why wasn't her mother home yet? Dinner doesn't take two hours.

She went upstairs and got ready for bed. She looked in the mirror and saw that her friend was gritting her teeth and shaking her head. "I know! Mrs. Wrenn is so hateful. It's so unfair!" she agreed with the little girl.

Instead of going to bed like she was told, she crept down the stairs. She decided to wait on the stairs for her mother. She couldn't be long now. It was chilly on the stairs so she pulled her nighty over her knees and wrapped her arms around herself to keep warm.

She could hear the Wrenns talking at the far end of the hall. She stopped breathing so she could hear what they were saying.

"That Rita! Out again, and on Christmas Eve for goodness' sake!"

"Didn't she say she'd be home by eight o'clock?" Mr. Wrenn asked.

"Well maybe she did and maybe she didn't, but regardless, you know she doesn't care what time she gets home. She tells that kid one thing, but does another. But really! To break her promises on Christmas Eve? What kind of mother is she?"

"Do you think she has a gift for her? Do you think she has a stocking at least?" Mr. Wrenn sounded worried.

"God only knows. I doubt it."

Cathy could hear Mrs. Wrenn coming down the hall so she jumped up and quietly ran up the stairs and back to the room. She pulled off her underpants and threw them into the corner and got in the bed. After her heart stopped racing, she lay there thinking about what Mrs. Wrenn said about her mother.

She hated how she talked about her, hated that she said her mother always breaks her promises. What did Mrs. Wrenn care? Then suddenly she heard a creak on the stairs. Had her mother come in so quietly that Cathy didn't hear her? She closed her eyes and pretended to be asleep; she was so happy that her mother was home. She knew she wouldn't let her down, she knew her mother would come home when she said she would. She waited for the familiar sound of her mother's cough, but instead she heard a sucking sound and with a start, she knew that it was Mrs. Wrenn coming up the stairs.

She closed her eyes even more tightly and braced herself for when Mrs. Wrenn would pull off the blanket to check to see if she had her underpants on. But instead she could hear Mrs. Wrenn creeping over to the kitchen table. She softly put something down and then crept back down the stairs. After a few moments, Cathy opened her eyes to make sure she was actually gone. When the coast was clear, she tiptoed over to the table to see what Mrs. Wrenn put there. She stopped dead in her tracks.

There on the table was a stocking with a wrapped gift inside. She didn't understand at first. How was the stocking already filled? Santa hadn't come yet. Kenny and Susan were still watching TV and everyone knew that Santa wouldn't come until all the people in the house were fast asleep.

Then it dawned on her. Mrs. Wrenn had filled the stocking, and she was hoping that when Cathy would wake up in the morning, she would think that Santa had left it for her. But now Cathy knew that maybe it was the parents that filled their children's stockings. Maybe Santa didn't do it at all? Maybe Santa didn't even exist?

Cathy didn't want to believe it but she couldn't think of any other reason why Mrs. Wrenn would do this. Did she know that Rita wouldn't be home in time to fill the stocking herself? Or that she wouldn't even have a gift for her? Was Mrs. Wrenn actually trying to be nice?

Instead of feeling thankful or believing that Mrs. Wrenn had one kind bone in her body, she felt a surge of frustration and anger; anger at her mother and utter disappointment and sadness to realize that there was no Santa Claus.

If she disliked Mrs. Wrenn before, she absolutely hated her now. She tiptoed back to bed and tried to fall asleep.

Cathy woke up on Christmas morning to the sound of her mother snoring right beside her. When her mother stayed out late, she would come home reeking of smoke and beer, and if she came home bumping into things, she often snored all night long. Cathy realized it was Christmas morning and opened her eyes. She desperately hoped there would be a gift from her mother on the table, but when she looked over to their little kitchen, all she could see was the wretched stocking that Mrs. Wrenn put there last night. She closed her eyes again and waited for her mother to wake up.

"Merry Christmas, Darlin'," Rita said as she sat up and stretched a while later. Cathy lay there pretending to be asleep. "Wake up sleepyhead, it's Christmas. Look what Santa brought you. He filled your stocking and left it over there on the table."

Cathy couldn't believe her ears. How stupid did her mother think she was? She opened her eyes and sat up and said, "That's not from Santa! Mrs. Wrenn did it! Now I know that there is no Santa."

"Hun, that's not true. Santa must have filled your stocking for you last night."

"No!" she started to raise her voice. "Mrs. Wrenn brought it up while you were out. You said you would be home and you weren't. They felt sorry for me because you forgot to get me a gift, so they put God knows what in some old stocking and pretended that Santa left it. But I was still awake! I saw her put it on the table!" Cathy was shaking now and her voice was getting louder and louder. "Where were you? Why were you so late? You promised me you would come home!" Cathy's voice was getting shrill and she thought her head was going to explode. Rita stared at her as if she'd lost her mind.

"I'm sorry, Hun! I lost track of time." Her eyes were wide and she looked like she was going to cry. Cathy didn't know what to do. Why was her mother crying? It was she who was so upset.

"Cathy, please stop yelling! You're scaring me." Rita buried her face in her hands. Cathy pursed her lips together and squeezed them until she was sure she could stop yelling. She closed her eyes and prayed to God to help her calm down. She heard her mother blow her nose, and when she opened her eyes, her mother was over at the counter putting the kettle on.

"Do you want a tea, Cathy-o?"

What happened to her mother's tears? How could she just turn them off like a faucet? She was such an actress!

Cathy was done. She was beyond trying to tell her mother how hurt she was. She didn't know how else to show her how sad and mad and frustrated she was.

They sat at the table drinking their tea in silence. They both stared at the stocking, but Cathy made no move to open the gift. When her tea was done, Cathy took the stocking and went to the garbage pail. She turned the stocking upside down and watched the gift fall in. She let go of the stocking too and then without another word went back to the bed and pulled the blanket over her head.

Elsie

CHAPTER EIGHTEEN

Stratford-Winter 1958

"Cathy? Ca-thy?" She heard a little voice right beside her ear. "Do you want to come to church with us?" It was Susan. Cathy pulled the blanket away from her face and looked at her. Susan never came up to the room, so Cathy was surprised to see her. "What are you doing up here?" she asked the little girl.

"My dad sent me up here to see if you want to come to our church this afternoon, for Christmas Service?"

Cathy was puzzled. The Wrenns knew that she was a Catholic. She couldn't go to some Protestant church.

She sat up and looked over at the table. Her mom had her head cradled in her arms on the table. She had fallen asleep. She must have had too much to drink last night, and because Cathy was so mad, her mother didn't dare get back in the bed with her. Cathy had no use for her when she was like this. She decided that she would go with the Wrenns. As much as she couldn't stand Mrs. Wrenn, at least Mr. Wrenn was always kind to her, and Kenny and Susan were OK too.

The church they went to was nowhere near as beautiful as St. Joseph's or Immaculate Conception, where she and her mom normally went when her mom wasn't sleeping in, but it was nice and quiet and Cathy was happy to have some time to pray.

She prayed to God that he would find a way for her to get back to Nana. She prayed that her mother would give up and just let her go back to where she belonged.

She blessed herself and sat in the pew and listened as the congregation sang their songs and as the pastor said his homily. She closed her eyes. She was so tired. A part of her was still so angry with her mom, but slowly, because she was sitting in church, she started to forgive her mother. She wished that her mother could be a better mom. She wished that they were happier. She wished that they could live somewhere else. When she got back to the house, she decided that she would talk to her mother to see if there was any way they could move away from the Wrenns. Maybe they could live with Uncle Doug and Aunt Elsie or Uncle Stan and Aunt Joanie? Anything to get out of that house.

When she got back to 28 Brant Street, her mother was waiting for her in the front hall. She already had her coat and boots on and she looked irritated.

"Where the heck were you?" she asked as she put her scarf on. "I've been waiting here for an hour!"

"I was at church with Susan. You were sleeping at the table, so I just left. I didn't think you'd care," answered Cathy.

"Care? Of course I care. Now turn right around and get outside. We were supposed to be at Doug and Elsie's already. The taxi's been waiting," she said as she shut the door and gently pushed Cathy towards the sidewalk. They got in the taxi and Cathy thought this would be a good time to ask her mom about moving out of the Wrenn's.

"Mom, I was thinking..." she started.

"I hope Elsie isn't mad. She hates it when we're late and I'm sure she put a lot of work into making a special dinner." Rita looked worried as she gazed out the window.

"I'm sure she'll be OK. She's used to us being late. But Mom, I wanted to ask you..." Cathy tried again.

"Where are those ASAs?" Rita mumbled as she rifled through her purse. "My head is killing me. Cathy, can you look through my purse and see if you can find the bottle? My head is paining me so badly I can't even see straight."

Cathy found the bottle, shook out two pills, and gave them to her mother. She knew that when her mother had these kinds of headaches there was no use in trying to talk to her. So she sighed and sat back against the seat and looked out her own window. This conversation would have to wait.

"Come in, my dears! Quick now before you let the winter in!" Aunt Elsie laughed as she closed the door behind them.

"Give me your coats and go and make yourselves comfortable in the living room."

Just hearing Aunt Elsie's voice and being in her cozy house made Cathy feel a little better.

"Sit down, sit down," Uncle Doug said, wildly gesturing towards the Chesterfield. "That's it, that's it. Put your feet up now."

The house was warm and it smelled of juicy turkey and baked pies. Cathy sat down and again she felt very tired; she just wanted to close her eyes and go to sleep.

The dining room table was set with all of Aunt Elsie's nicest things: linen napkins, crystal candle holders, and, of course, her very best china. The tree was beautifully decorated and there were Christmas cards on every surface in the room. Uncle Doug rolled in the serving cart and Cathy saw that it had colourful glass bowls filled with peanuts and pretzels and striped hard candy.

"Look, look here, help yourself." Uncle Doug flailed around. "C'mon, Cathy, take some peanuts." He pushed the bowl towards her before he ran back to the kitchen to get them a drink.

"Look at what Douglas got me for Christmas," Aunt Elsie said as she swooped into the room with a brand new fur coat that had a great big white collar and white cuffs. It went all the way to the floor, and as Aunt Elsie waltzed through the room it billowed out behind her. She had a big smile on her face and when Uncle Doug came back with the drinks, he smiled at her.

"What do ya think, Reet? You like it? You like it?" Uncle Doug said as he took his wife in his arms and danced her around the room.

"Oh, Elsie! What a beautiful coat!" Rita said as she admired her sister-in-law from the couch.

Cathy smiled at her aunt and uncle and thought about how cute they were. They loved each other so much and although many people thought Uncle Doug was a little annoying, there was no one else in the world for Aunt Elsie. She was so proud of her Douglas and in her eyes, he was perfect.

During their quiet Christmas dinner, Cathy slowly started to relax. The sad and angry emotions of the day eventually flowed out of her and she was left feeling depleted and exhausted.

They had their tea and dessert on the couch, and after she was done Cathy laid her head in her mother's lap. Her mother smoothed the hair back from her face and softly rubbed her back. Cathy tried to stay awake and listen to their quiet conversation, but the peacefulness of the room and the ticking of the mantle clock made it impossible. She fell into a deep, restful sleep.

Myra (second from left) and Cathy

CHAPTER NINETEEN

Stratford-Winter/Spring 1959

Winter was bitter cold that year. Stratford was known as the snowbelt and if other cities in Southern Ontario got a few inches of snow, Stratford got a foot. The snow banks were piled so high it was impossible for people to back out of their driveways without almost getting hit. Mr. Wrenn was out shoveling every day and it took extra-long for Cathy to get to school in the mornings. The reason it took so long was because instead of trying to walk on the ice-covered sidewalks, it was much more fun to walk up and over the snow banks that formed along the roadside.

Cathy would pretend that she was a mountain climber and she would carefully dig her toes into the side of the bank and climb all the way to the top. Once she arrived at the summit, she would wave her arm as if she were carrying a big flag, and then she would start her descent all the way to the bottom. Sometimes she would turn around and go down on her belly. Other times she would just slide down on her bum and land at the bottom with a bump. She'd smile to herself and prepare for the next big climb. She did this all the way to school—up and down, up and down.

During recess, she and Myra would get all bundled up and head into the yard. They were making an ice rink. They would spend the whole recess moving the snow to the side to form a rectangle. This was really hard because they didn't have any shovels or anything, so they had to use their hands. Once they got the snow cleared, they realized that maybe they needed water to form the ice. They had no idea where to get water, so they decided to just pretend that it was icy. Then they would make believe that they were wearing beautiful white ice skates. The girls would shuffle around the rectangle with their hands clasped behind their backs and they would jump in the air knowing that all the other kids in the yard were impressed with their skills. Cathy imagined that she was wearing an ice-blue leotard with a short, ruffled skirt. She pictured herself with long hair all done up in a tight bun, and blue eyeshadow and lipstick to make her look theatrical.

When the bell would ring, the girls would get in line in front of the doors. The nuns were very particular about the students keeping quiet and staying in single file before they were allowed back in the school. All afternoon, sitting at her desk, Cathy would dream about her ice rink and about how excited she was to get back out there again the next day.

One day, after arriving at 28 Brant Street after school let out, it was almost dark and she was freezing. Her arms and legs felt wobbly from all the mountain climbing she did on the way home, and she couldn't wait to get in the house and put the kettle on for a nice hot cup of tea. She was just starting to peel off her wet, frozen coat when Mrs. Wrenn came out of the kitchen.

"Cathy, I need you to run down to the corner store and get me some milk. Mr. Wrenn forgot to get it on his way home and we need it for breakfast tomorrow," Mrs. Wrenn said as she handed Cathy some money.

Cathy noticed Kenny and Susan's boots were on the mat and she could hear the TV in the living room. Cathy wondered why Mrs. Wrenn didn't ask Kenny to go. He was older than Cathy and he must have already been home for over an hour. He only had to walk about 10 minutes from his school, and it took Cathy almost 45 minutes to get back from St. Joe's. Plus, with all the mountain climbing it probably took her more than an hour.

"Go now, please!" Mrs. Wrenn said as she stood waiting impatiently with the door open. "Hurry up, it's getting cold in here."

The last thing in the world that Cathy wanted to do was go back outside, but she couldn't say anything; she could never say anything.

With a sigh, she went back down the stairs and up the road. It was dark and the wind had picked up. Her feet were wet and her cheeks were sore with windburn.

Why do I have to go? I don't even get to hardly have any milk. Why didn't she make Kenny go, for God's sake?

She was sick to death of the unfairness of it all. No one cared about her. Mr. Wrenn never argued with his wife about the way she treated her. Kenny and Susan acted as if she was a second-class citizen and her mother was too tired, too hungover or too worried about Walter to even listen to what Cathy had to say. She fought back the tears, but her throat was tightening and it was hard to swallow. She wanted to scream, but all the neighbours would think she was a nut case if she did.

She was sick of keeping it all in, but there was no one to talk to, and for some reason she just couldn't bring herself to tell her aunts and uncles about her miserable life at the Wrenn's. Nobody would say anything against Rita. Not that she would be rude to them, but she was the oldest and it seemed like all of her siblings didn't feel it was their place to question her; the way she lived her life, or the way she mothered Cathy. Besides, Cathy always put a smile on her face when she was with the family. She tried to appear calm, cool, and collected at all times, just like Nana wanted.

Humph! Well she guessed she fooled them all, didn't she?

She was becoming quite the little actress, just like her mom. If she acted happy and content, the aunts and uncles just assumed she was, and although they always asked her how school was and how her friends were, they never asked any real questions like, are you getting enough sleep, or enough food? Are you being treated well?

She felt alone. She felt unloved and uncared for. Tears were falling down her cold cheeks and for a moment the tears felt nice and warm, but she quickly wiped them away because she knew they would soon freeze.

She got to the store and pulled open the frosty door. The little bell tinkled and Cathy was happy to see that Mrs. Lewis was working at the counter. She recognized Cathy but seemed surprised to see her tonight.

"My dear! What are you doing out in this weather?" She leaned over the counter and smiled down at Cathy.

"I have to get some milk, Mrs. Lewis. They need it for their breakfast in the morning," Cathy said quietly.

Her nose had started running. Mrs. Lewis handed her a tissue and said, "Wait right there sweetheart, I'll get a bottle for you." As she walked down the aisle to the cooler, Cathy saw her shake her head as if she were wondering why Mrs. Wrenn would send an eight-year-old child out on a night like this.

After Mrs. Lewis rang in the milk and slid the bottle across the counter she said, "Here dear, why don't you pick out some penny candy for yourself."

Cathy started to shake her head because she had to make sure Mrs. Wrenn got all of her change back.

"It's on me," Mrs. Lewis smiled encouragingly.

For some reason, Cathy felt like bawling. She would be horrified if Mrs. Lewis saw her crying, but she knew it was going to be impossible to fight back the tears. She sniffed and coughed and started choosing candies to go in the little bag the storekeeper gave her. Mrs. Lewis silently placed another tissue on the counter and looked up at the door as another customer came in. Cathy quickly took the tissue and dried her tears and wiped her nose. She didn't think Mrs. Lewis saw her crying. She really was becoming a good actress.

"Thank you very much, Mrs. Lewis," Cathy waved good-bye and went back out into the wind and snow.

Cathy's Ninth Birthday Party.
(Cathy is far left with just her crown showing)

CHAPTER TWENTY

Stratford-Spring 1959

Two months had gone by and the winter snow had melted and the ice rink at the school had turned to water. The roadside mountains became foothills and then small ridges and then finally little streams draining into the gutter. Snow boots were replaced with shoes, and hats and mitts were put away for another year. The grass was starting to grow, and the birds were flying back from their vacation in Florida.

It was April once again and Cathy's ninth birthday was coming up. She was allowed to invite five of her friends. Of course she invited Elaine and Myra, and Mrs. Wrenn made her invite Kenny and Susan. She didn't understand why, if she was having her party at Aunt Elsie's, she should have to invite them. But, of course, her mother didn't say anything when she complained, so Susan and Kenny were there too.

Once again, Aunt Elsie went all out. She had her best white linen cloth on her dining room table and a serving tray full of cookies as a centre piece. At every place setting she had placed paper firecrackers that the kids had no idea what to do with.

"Sit down now children, we're going to play a game," Aunt Elsie sang as the children took their spots.

"Alright, Cathy, you take the special chair, and you'll see why in a minute. Now you go ahead and open the firecracker." Aunt Elsie showed her how to take the two tabs at either end of the firecracker and pull as hard as she could. After a sulphur smelling bang, a tiny package shot out of the cracker. When Cathy opened it up, she unfolded a paper crown. It was pink and had jewels glued to it, and on it was written "Queen for a Day". She laughed and put it on her head.

"See now? Cathy my darling, you're the queen for a day!" All the children laughed and opened their firecrackers too. They also had little crowns, but not as fancy as Cathy's.

Aunt Elsie bought cherry-flavoured Kist soda and each child got to have their own bottle. She also had a deck of cards and taught them all how to play Go Fish, and then she had them blindfolded and turned around trying to pin the tail on the donkey. The kids were smiling and laughing and having a wonderful time.

While the party was going on, Rita and Doug sat in the living room smoking cigarettes and talking about the family in Cape Breton. They hadn't been down home for a couple years and they were thinking of planning a trip there this summer.

"I sure miss Daddy," Rita said to her brother as she blew out a stream of smoke.

"Yep," Doug said with a typical East Coast intake of air. "Wonder how he's doing?"

They were both very close to their father, and as happy as they were after moving to Ontario, they missed their parents very much. They both sent money down home regularly, but they also knew it was never enough.

Rosie had come up to Ontario a few months ago, but Marlene, Janey, and Francis still lived in the house. Rita and Doug grew silent thinking about the little girls and the circumstances around why they lived there. Lord knew that their mother had raised enough kids without having to worry about two more, but no one could say no to Daddy, especially not his wife. And if he wanted to bring those two girls into his house, he would do it, but it didn't make it any easier to put food on the table.

The last time Rita saw her mother, she worried about how tired she looked. Her mother didn't seem as strong as she used to be and she always had aches and pains in her side. Daddy also seemed older than his 62 years, and although she didn't like to admit it, she knew that he drank too much and too often.

She looked at Doug and knew from the look on his face that he worried too.

"Come on everyone, let's sing 'Happy Birthday'!" Aunt Elsie paraded around the living room holding the cake lit with nine candles. She looked at her husband and sister-in-law and gestured them into the kitchen.

They finished their song, clapped, and wished Cathy a happy birthday. Rita cut the cake and handed the plates to all the children. She smiled at her daughter and touched her cheek. Cathy smiled up at her mom and said, "How do you like my crown? I'm the Queen!" She laughed with Elaine and Myra and then they ate their cake and finished their Kist.

Nana and Papa

CHAPTER TWENTY-ONE

Stratford/Cape Breton-Spring 1959

"Rita! The telephone is for you," Mrs. Wrenn called from the front hall.

It had been three weeks since Cathy's birthday and Rita and Cathy were up in their room eating a simple supper of cold cuts and buns. They were just about to eat the cinnamon rolls Rita bought on the way home when they heard Mrs. Wrenn's screechy voice coming up the stairs. Rita looked at Cathy and wondered who could be calling. She had just talked to Joanie yesterday, so she didn't think it would be her again. "Rita!"

"Coming!" Rita ran down the stairs and took the phone from Mrs. Wrenn. Cathy followed her down because Mrs. Wrenn sounded extra urgent and Cathy wanted to see who was calling.

"Hello? Hi Molly, how're you doing?" Rita smiled at Cathy. She listened for a few minutes and then the colour drained out of her face.

"What? No!" Rita slumped onto the bench beside the telephone table. Cathy's eyes widened.

She could hear a sound. It started out low and then got louder and louder, it sounded like a wounded animal. She realized it was her mother.

"Noooooooooo…." The animal sound turned into racking sobs. Rita looked up at her daughter.

"Daddy's dead!" she moaned as she dropped the telephone and buried her face in her hands.

Eventually Mrs. Wrenn and Cathy were able to guide Rita back up the steps and they laid her down on the bed. Mrs. Wrenn got a cold cloth and placed it on Rita's forehead. Cathy had never seen Mrs. Wrenn do anything like that before. She almost seemed like a human or something. Finally, Mrs. Wrenn went downstairs and Cathy crawled into the bed beside her mother. Rita had stopped crying, but she wouldn't open her eyes. Cathy tried to hold her mother but all she was able to do was press the side of her face against her mother's tear-stained cheek.

"What happened to Papa?" she whispered in her mother's ear.

"Oh, Cathy, I'll never get over it. Molly said he got hit by a train."

"Hit by a train? How did that happen?"

"No one seems to know. He was late coming home from work and he was walking the tracks like he always did. Molly said they waited and waited for him until it was almost midnight and then they went to bed thinking that he fell asleep during one of his poker games. In the morning, Leo O'Neil knocked on their door. Mama almost fell over because Leo hadn't darkened their door since years, but when she saw the look on his face, she knew something was wrong." She started to cry again and Cathy jumped up and got her some Kleenex. Rita sat up and blew her nose. Cathy sat beside her on the side of the bed.

"Leo said he was going to work in the cemetery when he saw Daddy lying in the ditch. He ran up to him hoping that he'd only passed out, but when he got near, he knew Daddy'd been hit by a train."

Rita wrapped her arms around Cathy and pulled her close. She rocked her daughter back and forth and sobbed into her hair. Cathy felt like she had been in a trance ever since the phone rang, but now, in her mother's arms, she realized that her beloved Papa was gone. Hit by a train on the way home from work. She felt as if her heart had been ripped out of her chest. She broke down and cried harder than she had in a long time.

She let her mother hold her, and they rocked each other back and forth for what seemed like hours. Eventually, they pulled the covers over their heads, wrapped their arms around each other, and fell asleep.

They left the next day for Cape Breton. They barely had time to let the school know that Cathy would be missing class until the end of the year. As soon as they arrived at Nana's house, Rita fell into her mother's arms. Marlene and Janey ran to Cathy and they hugged her and hugged her. Their little faces were red and blotchy with all of the tears they had been crying over the past couple of days.

After the funeral, the whole family gathered at the house. Uncle Doug had arrived but hadn't said a word to anyone. He was sitting in his daddy's chair by the woodstove, just staring at the floor. Cathy knew he was hit hard because he was his daddy's favourite son and he loved his father like crazy. Nana was sitting in her rocker with her prayer book and her rosary. The priest had come back to the house with them, and he was sitting with Nana trying to console her. She didn't say anything and she wasn't crying. She just kept praying and rocking and rocking and praying. She stayed like that for two days.

Eventually, the house got back to normal. Aunt Alice and Johnny Ryan went back home with their kids. Aunt Tussie and her two went back to Jimmy, and Francis headed downtown to drink his sadness away. After hugging and kissing Cathy, Marlene, and Janey, Big Molly went back home with Rolfe and their daughter, Little Molly.

Cathy's mom was sitting beside Nana, and they were both saying their prayers over and over. Cathy felt like she needed to get out of the house; Marlene and Janey were getting antsy too so she said, "Come on girls, let's go play." They instantly jumped up and followed Cathy out the door.

First they ran over the tracks and up the road as far as they could go, and when the road ended, they did a big circle through the field and the scrubby bushes back towards the house. When Cathy ran over the tracks for the second time, she got such a shiver down her spine, she veered away from the house and went the opposite way down the road.

Cathy didn't know where they were going. All she knew was that she wanted to run. The three girls ran and ran until they couldn't catch their breath. They ran all the way down to the end of 1B road, past the mine that Papa worked at, and all the way to the cliff. They fell to the ground, huffing and puffing and leaning on each other. They sat together in the tall grass not saying a single word. All three of them looked out across the ocean and watched the seagulls dive for fish. The sky was clear and the ocean was blue and the sun was warm on their faces.

Cathy lay back in the grass and watched as a light breeze blew the puffy clouds across the sky. The clouds were slowly changing shape as they went, and Cathy swallowed back her tears when she realized that one of them looked a bit like a strutting rooster.

Joanie, Alma, Doug, Elsie and Cathy

CHAPTER TWENTY-TWO

Stratford-Summer 1959

Cathy and Rita stayed in Cape Breton for a whole month, and even though Cathy begged to stay longer, her mother told her that she needed to get back to Ontario and back to work.

"Don't forget that Mrs. Wrenn keeps charging me rent while we're gone, Hun," she explained. "So I need to get back to work and make some money."

Cathy could tell that her mother didn't want to leave Cape Breton either. She was still so sad about her father and being with her brothers and sisters and her mother made her feel better. Even though Cathy thought this would be a good time to ask her mom if she could stay for the rest of the summer, she couldn't bring herself to add more stress. She knew her mother needed her, and how could she send her back to Mrs. Wrenn's all alone?

Life in Stratford was much more bearable in the summer. When summer vacation began, Cathy missed her school friends and missed being able to get out of the Wrenn's house every day, but when it was warm out, you could go anywhere in Stratford. Cathy would often wake up in the morning, bypass the kitchen and the Wrenns, and head straight out the door and down the steps. She would walk through the backyard and over the tracks towards the train station. Sometimes she would sit on the bench on the platform and watch the trains go by.

Big, heavy freight trains would come chugging down the tracks blowing smoke and making a racket, but these slow-moving trains didn't stop at the station. Sometimes Cathy would jump up and wave at the conductor and he would wave back. Passenger trains would come whooshing in with the whistle blaring and then screech to a halt to let the passengers out. They would often be smiling and happy because they would either be coming from out of town to go to the Festival, or they would just be spending the day uptown shopping and going to the restaurants.

Then more passengers would board the train, most likely headed for London or Toronto, and the doors would shut, the whistle would blow, and off it would go. Cathy longed for the day that she would be old enough to buy a ticket and board the train. No one would be able to stop her then. She would stay on the train until it got all the way to Cape Breton, and she would never come back to Stratford again.

After the excitement of the train station, she would make her way across town and down to the river. There were always lots of people around; men and women dressed up for the Festival; moms and dads with their children going for walks and looking for a cool spot in the shade for a picnic; children playing at the park or heading over to the pool for a swim; and sweethearts holding hands, walking along the river, and stopping at the park benches to steal kisses.

The swans had been paraded from where they stayed all winter down to the river where they spent the warm months swimming up and down the Avon. To Cathy they looked majestic; as if maybe they had been kings and queens in their past lives, and they would look down their noses at the silly people gawking at them from the river's edge.

When she was done her visit with the swans, she would make her way back through town toward City Hall. It was such a beautiful building and sometimes she would sit on the steps and watch the people go by. If she had any money, which wasn't often, she would go to the famous French fry wagon and buy the smallest container they had of hot, greasy, salty fries. She would savor each one and eat them as slowly as possible so that they would last until she got back to the tracks. She would make a stop at the station again to dump the container and go to the bathroom before walking as slowly as she could back to 28 Brant Street.

This summer, Kenny and Susan were away visiting family, and since her mother and Mr. Wrenn had to work every day, Cathy was stuck with Mrs. Wrenn. Cathy very rarely made an appearance back at the house during the day, but if she had nowhere else to go, she would sometimes find herself sitting at the front of the house on the steps.

The day was a real scorcher. Another thing about Stratford was that it was hot, hot, hot in the summer. Down home, you were never that hot because there was always an ocean breeze to cool you down, but in Stratford it was very still and humid. She was especially hot now after walking around town all morning; the sun was beating down on her head giving her a headache as she waited on the steps in hopes that her friend, Elaine, was around.

She had already knocked on Elaine's door but there was no answer. Maybe she was out with her family and would be home soon. Cathy sat on the steps for a while but couldn't take the heat any longer. She went into the yard and, hoping for some shade, stood under the scrawny tree kicking twigs and maple keys around. Without any relief from the heat of the sun, she decided to walk up the road and then back down again scanning the sidewalk for any kids that wanted to play. It seemed like everyone was away, either visiting relatives, out with their families, or away at summer camp.

Cathy imagined herself in Goderich at Mrs. Allen's cottage. What she wouldn't give to put her toes in the water of Lake Huron right now. She was getting bored and she wished she had a skipping rope or some chalk to play with. The last thing she wanted to do was go back into the house, so even if she played with a stick or something, it would be better than the dark, stuffy living room with the noisy bird.

"Cathy!" Mrs. Wrenn must have seen her hanging around outside and now she wanted her to come in. Oh, why didn't she just keep walking up the road? She should have gone to Joanie and Stan's or to the park or back down to the river.

"Cathy! Come in here right now!" Mrs. Wrenn yelled from the door.

With a sigh she dropped her stick and went up the steps and into the house. Mrs. Wrenn was standing there squinting at her.

"I can't stand this heat. I'm melting and I need something to cool me off." Cathy noticed rivulets of sweat dripping down the sides of Mrs. Wrenn's face. She gave a bit of a shudder and looked down at the floor.

"Go to the store and get me a cold bottle of ginger ale and an ice cream cone. I don't care what flavour you get, just get me two scoops of whatever they have." She shoved a few bills at Cathy's face. "And don't forget to bring me back all of the change."

She always brought back all of the change. She didn't need to be reminded every single time. Cathy gritted her teeth, turned, and went back down the stairs.

Ugh…it was so hot! Cathy hoped for a breeze or a cloud to cover the sun for a little bit. Her headache was getting worse and she was starting to sweat. She got to the store and was disappointed that Mrs. Lewis wasn't working today. She ordered the ginger ale and the ice cream and paid the man behind the counter. The cold bottle of ginger ale felt nice and cold in her hands. She held it against her forehead and it soothed her aching head.

She crossed the street to the other side of the road and started walking down the sidewalk back to the house. She felt a cool drip on her hand and looked to see that the ice cream was melting. She quickly licked the ice cream off her finger. After another minute she felt another drip. She licked her finger again. Now the ice cream was melting more quickly and to stop it, Cathy had to lick the ice cream itself. Once she licked the one side and stopped it from dripping, she saw that the other side was dripping too. She quickly licked it. The more she licked it, the more it dripped! Soon the ice cream cone was getting smaller and smaller. She started running. She couldn't let Mrs. Wrenn know that she licked her ice cream cone. God only knows what would happen to her if she found out. The ice cream dripped and dripped, but she didn't dare lick it again. It was already half the size. She ran up the two steps and pushed the door open. Mrs. Wrenn was standing there with her hands on her hips.

"Well, that took you long enough. What did you do, crawl to the store?" She took the ginger ale bottle out of Cathy's hand and looked at the ice cream. Cathy stood perfectly still and looked down at her shoes, waiting for Mrs. Wrenn to start hollering. When Cathy finally looked up, Mrs. Wrenn was eyeing the ice cream suspiciously.

"Well, my lord! They're making the cones smaller and smaller every year." She took the cone, took one more look at Cathy, and walked back into the kitchen.

Cathy smiled to herself and thought, *Well, it looks like we got away with that one!*

(Back left to right) Doug, Elsie, Ted and Rita
Ted's girlfriend with Cathy, Johnny MacMillan, Alma and Mickey

CHAPTER TWENTY-THREE

Stratford-End of Summer 1959

The hot, humid summer was coming to an end and everyone was coming back from summer vacation. Cathy was relieved because as much as Kenny and Susan got on her nerves, it was a lot better having them around than it was being lonely and bored all summer. Since the Wrenns didn't have a car, (there was only one family on the whole street that had one), their driveway was empty. Georgie English's dad had the loan of a boat for the summer and he'd arranged to store it in Mr. Wrenn's driveway for a few months. The boat turned out to be more fun than the jungle gym at the park.

Cathy, Kenny, Georgie, Elaine, and Susan would spend hours pretending they were pirates on a pirate ship. Kenny was the captain, of course, and Georgie was the first mate. Cathy and Elaine had to spend a lot of time "swabbing the decks" and poor Susan had to spend most of her time in the "galley" preparing meals for the crew.

"Har there, matey!" Kenny would growl over and over. They all practiced talking like pirates and they often dissolved into giggles whenever anyone was sent up to the "poop deck" to keep an eye on the lazy crew. If the captain was too busy looking over his maps, he'd send his first mate to the poop deck to help with navigation.

Georgie, in his best pirate voice would say, "I'll get me-self up to the poop deck. Here I go, up to the poop deck." And every time he said it, the rest of the kids would fall down laughing. If the first mate or the captain got a feeling that they were being followed, they would bellow to the crew,

"Get ye up to the crow's nest and use yer peepers to see what ya can see!" The girls would pretend to climb the rope ladder up to the crow's nest and look all around to find the dratted enemy ship.

They would spend all day out in the ship. They made pirate costumes for themselves out of old clothes they found in the basement, and Mr. Wrenn would make them all eye patches and whittle a few swords out of wood for them to share.

Sometimes, if her mother was home, she would make them all peanut butter and jam sandwiches to eat on their ship. The kids had so much fun and were so disappointed when the sun went down and they had to go in for supper. Cathy could hardly sleep at night thinking about all the fun they would have the next day on their pirate ship.

Cathy was shocked when her mom came home early one evening. She said that Walter was away visiting friends so instead of coming home late, she came home right after work. The two of them made grilled cheese sandwiches on their little hot plate, and instead of eating in the cramped apartment, Rita thought it would be fun to eat outside. It was a warm evening and the Wrenns were out somewhere, so Cathy and Rita got to sit on the steps and eat their supper in peace and quiet.

The sun was warm on their faces, but there was a gentle breeze to keep them cool. Cathy smiled up at her mother and moved closer to her so that their knees touched.

Rita put her arm around her daughter's shoulders and said, "C'mon, Hun, let's walk to the store and get some ice cream for dessert." She stood up and brushed the crumbs off her skirt.

Cathy was surprised. It was very rare that she and her mom did anything like this. She took their plates and ran them into the kitchen. She quickly rinsed them and put them away so that Mrs. Wrenn wouldn't be mad about dirty dishes in the sink.

The sun was starting to set and the crickets were chirping. Cathy loved this time of the year and was happy that they were walking slowly so that they could enjoy every minute of it. She was excited to see that Mrs. Lewis was working the counter.

"Hi, Mrs. Lewis," Cathy said with a proud smile. "This is my mom."

Mrs. Lewis inclined her head to Rita. "Yes, I know who you are. You work at the hospital. I didn't know you were little Cathy's mom."

Rita smiled and said, "Oh. Yes. Pleased to meet you. How do you know my daughter?"

"Because she's constantly here buying milk, or ginger ale, or ice cream for that woman you live with, Mrs. Wrenn." Mrs. Lewis did not smile back at Rita.

Cathy noticed that her mother's face got red and she looked uncomfortable.

"Let's order our ice cream, Mom." Cathy wasn't sure what was happening but she felt a tension in the air.

Once they left the store and walked back to the house, they relaxed again. They sat close together on the steps and finished their ice cream. It was a warm and peaceful evening and Cathy was so happy to be with her mom that she put her head on her shoulder. Rita smiled and patted Cathy's knee and the two of them watched the sun go down.

The next morning, Rita and Cathy had a sponge bath in their room, got dressed, and did their hair. Everyone was getting together at Doug and Elsie's for lunch because Aunt Elsie invited her brother Ted for a visit. Cathy met Ted a few times before and she thought he was a very nice man. They were also having another visitor for lunch, a man named Johnny MacMillan. Cathy knew who he was. He had been at their parties before and everyone liked when he showed up because he kept them all in stitches with his silly antics.

It was another beautiful day, but a little cooler, so Rita and Cathy wore their coats, and instead of calling a taxi, they decided to walk. Uncle Doug and Aunt Elsie moved last year to a new house on Easson Street and although it was a long walk, the day was just too perfect to be in a car.

The house was full when they arrived: Uncle Doug and Aunt Elsie, Uncle Mickey and Aunt Alma, Ted, Johnny MacMillan, and a beautiful woman Cathy had never met before. Apparently, she was Ted's new girlfriend and when her mom shook the woman's hand, she didn't seem overly happy with this new situation. Ted had always been single, and Aunt Elsie often tried to get her brother and her sister-in-law to go on a date, but Rita was still trying to keep Walter's attention, so she never took Ted up on any of his offers to take her out. Now with the arrival of this new woman, time and choices had run out for Rita.

They were the last ones to arrive, and as soon as they did Aunt Elsie jumped up and grabbed her camera.

"Perfect! Everyone's here now so we can take a photograph!" She herded everyone outside where it was bright and sunny. Cathy didn't know anyone who liked to take photos more than her Aunt Elsie.

Rita had already taken off her hat and coat, but just before she could put them back on, Johnny MacMillan took them from her and put them on himself. He was a little man so the coat fit, but when he put the hat on it looked like a fuzzy white wig. Then, smiling at Cathy, he took the little purse she'd brought with her.

"This will look perfect with my new outfit," he said in a girlish voice. He turned around and around, showing off his new coat and then he blew a kiss at Uncle Mickey and batted his eye lashes at Uncle Doug.

"Take that off, you. You look like a fool!" Uncle Doug laughed as he lit a cigarette.

Everyone was laughing as Aunt Elsie aimed the camera. "Smile!" She sang as she clicked away.

Cathy noticed that Ted had his arms around Rita and he was squeezing her tight. Rita was smiling and loving every moment of the attention. His girlfriend saw too, but she didn't seem to care as she grabbed Cathy and put her on her lap. She tickled her and told her what a pretty girl she was. Cathy liked her instantly and spent the rest of the evening sitting with her and listening to her stories.

She was an actress and she was currently in a play that was on at the Festival. Last night was the last show and she and Ted would be leaving town in the morning. Before Rita and Cathy left to go home, the lady pulled Cathy aside and opened her hand. In it, she had a gold tube of lipstick.

"This is for you, pretty girl. Whenever you want to play dress up, you can put this red lipstick on and pretend you are a great actress, like me." She put the lipstick into Cathy's purse for her, gave her a big hug, and promised to look her up the next time she was in town.

Cathy never saw the lady again, but for the rest of her life, she always kept a tube of lipstick in her purse for whenever she wanted to play dress up.

Reg Larion

CHAPTER TWENTY-FOUR

Stratford-Early Fall 1959

Her mother was still dating Walter "Glass Whiskey", and Cathy thought it was obvious he wasn't going to marry her any time soon. One fall evening Walter came over, and he and her mother were sitting on the steps in front of the house because Mrs. Wrenn wouldn't allow him inside. Cathy sat in her usual secret spot on the stairs in the shadows of the house, so she could watch them through the screen door and listen to what they were saying. She always hoped those overheard conversations would be talk about marriage and moving to a nice little house and about Walter maybe becoming her dad.

This particular evening, Cathy's ears perked up because she heard them say her name.

"Rita, I've told you before how I feel about this," Walter said. "I'm not going to change my mind."

"But Walter, I thought you loved me. We've been together for more than five years; how much longer do I have to wait?" Rita put her hand on his arm. He shook it off and lit a cigarette.

"Listen, I am not going to take on another man's responsibility. I never signed up for that. When I met you, you were single and available and I had every intention of marrying you. But then you brought Cathy back here and everything changed."

"No, Walter, nothing's changed. Cathy's a sweet girl, I thought you liked her."

"I like her Rita, but she's not mine and I'm not going to pay for her. Now like I've told you before, get a hold of Reg and tell him to be a man and pay for his kid!" He threw the butt onto the sidewalk.

Reg? Reg Larion? What did Walter mean "pay for his kid"?

"You know I'm not going to do that, Walter. If Reg wanted to acknowledge his daughter and help take care of her, he would have done it by now. I'm not going to beg him." Her mom's voice sounded choked.

What were they saying? That Reg Larion was her father?? Cathy had always heard the aunts and uncles whispering about the Larions, and she even heard Nana and Molly talking about

Reg one time. She knew he was Frank Larion's brother, Kay's brother-in-law, but she never guessed in a million years that he was her father.

Cathy wasn't really able to comprehend this information. She couldn't connect the dots in her head. It was true that she always wondered who her father was, but something in her brain would stop her from thinking about it. She was afraid to ask. She was afraid to find out who her mother had been with, who the father was that didn't want her. She saw her birth certificate once and under the title of father it just said "none." None. No one. That meant that whoever he was, he didn't want her.

With all the misery she had in her life already, she couldn't let herself think about this man who didn't love her or want to care for her. She had enough of those feelings without adding the knowledge that she had a father out there who had abandoned her.

And to make it all worse, it wasn't a stranger, it was Reg Larion! No wonder her Uncle Frank was always acting so weird around her. He knew that she was his niece, not just through Aunt Kay, but through his own brother for God's sake!

This was too much. She couldn't deal with this. She could hear her mother crying and it just made her sick. She was sick of her mother's whining and carrying on. What did her mother have to be sad about? She wanted to run down the stairs and fling the screen door open. She wanted to yell at her mother and tell her to shut up! Stop your crying, you stupid article! She screamed inside her head. I'm the one who should be crying!

Instead she ran up the stairs to their room. She threw herself onto the bed and buried her face into the stained pillow.

She didn't realize that she had fallen asleep. It was dark and her mother was snoring beside her. A wave of sadness came over her as she remembered what Walter said. It hit her that not only did Reg Larion not want her, but Walter didn't want her either. Then another wave; this one bigger than the first. She knew that when she was only 18 months old, her mother didn't want her either. She had sent her to live with Nana. Cathy never really thought about why she lived with Nana all those years, but now she knew; her mother didn't want her then, and she probably didn't want her now. Cathy suddenly realized that her mother's life would have been easier if Cathy wasn't born at all.

She curled herself into a little ball. She felt like she was in physical pain. All the muscles in her body were clenched and her mouth was open but no sound was coming out.

After a little while her body finally relaxed and she sobbed silently into her pillow. She cried harder than she ever did in her life, but no one would have known, because she was silent, she didn't make a sound. Inside, the little girl's heart was breaking apart, and it would never be whole again.

Cathy

CHAPTER TWENTY-FIVE

Stratford-Late Fall 1959

Cathy walked slowly from school to 28 Brant Street. Just before she left the classroom, her teacher, the Sister, had given her a letter. The letter was addressed to Rita Barron. Cathy wasn't sure what was written in the letter but she had a clue that it had something to do with her bad marks. Lately she was very tired during the day at school. Her eyes often felt heavy and it was hard to concentrate on what the Sister was saying. Sometimes when she was writing in her workbook, she would jerk awake and look at her writing and realize the line of ink was drifting down the page. Had she just fallen asleep? Other times, she would hear Sister saying her name and again, she'd realized that she'd been dozing, and the kids were laughing at her.

After school, Sister asked her to stay behind. Cathy was nervous because she had never been in trouble at school before and she didn't know what to expect.

"Cathy dear, is everything all right with you?" Sister asked her gently.

"Yes, Sister," Cathy responded.

"How is your mother? Are you eating properly?"

"Yes." Cathy didn't know what to say. Should she be honest and say that life was miserable once again? That any happy memories she had from the summer had faded away with the sun? Should she tell her that she hardly saw her mother these days? That she came home long after Cathy was asleep and left before she woke up. That she went out almost every Friday and Saturday night and was so hungover on Sundays that she didn't even go to church. That she just laid in bed all day taking pills and complaining about her headaches.

Should she tell the nun that Mrs. Wrenn was creeping up the stairs again every morning to see if she was "behaving"? Should she tell her that when Kenny and Susan watched TV, she had to do the dishes, dust the living room, and clean all the baseboards? That she had to go to bed early while the Wrenn kids stayed up late? Should she tell her that she felt totally alone, unloved, and uncared for?

No, she would never tell her those things. Those things she kept to herself. Those things she only shared with the little girl in the mirror. The little girl in the mirror was the only one who understood that she was completely miserable.

"OK dear, well you run along home then, but please give this letter to your mother." The sister looked worried as she passed the letter to Cathy. Cathy took it, put it in her book bag, knowing she would never give it to her mom, and walked out of the classroom.

On the way home, she couldn't stop thinking about how much she hated living at the Wrenn's. It had been almost five years since they moved in. She thought they would have had their own place by now.

When she finally arrived at 28 Brant Street, she felt exhausted. She went in the door and started to take her coat off. She was planning on going straight up the stairs and falling into bed when Mrs. Wrenn came down the hall, gesturing to Cathy to go back out.

"Cathy, you don't need to be in here right now. Go outside and play. I don't want you lazing around upstairs like you did yesterday."

Cathy was about to protest, but she just didn't have the energy. She shrugged her coat back on and turned around and went out the door. She walked up the street and walked back down. No one was out playing. It was cold and dark and most kids were in their houses with their parents. They were probably sitting at their kitchen tables, eating cookies, and drinking milk. Their fathers were probably helping them with their homework while their mothers were cooking supper.

Cathy sighed and looked down the street to see if maybe her mother was coming home. It certainly wasn't likely; Rita hadn't been home before dark for months. Cathy guessed that she was trying her best to make Walter marry her. She seemed desperate, and the harder she tried, the more he kept his distance. Cathy knew now that when her mother wasn't with Walter, she was at the Dominion hotel uptown. God only knew what she did up there all evening, but when she came home, she always smelled like beer and cigarettes. Cathy didn't know how her mother could go to bed so late every night but still manage to wake up so early every morning. How was she able to work all day in the Laundry with the headaches she always had?

It had been almost an hour that Cathy was outside. It was damp and cold and she was starving. She just wanted to go to their room and make some tea and toast. Maybe Mrs. Wrenn would let her in now. She walked up the steps and pulled on the door handle. It wouldn't budge. She tried again. Maybe it was stuck. But it wouldn't open. She stopped, took a deep breath, and tried again. It was locked. She couldn't believe it was locked. Mrs. Wrenn had locked her out.

Cathy had nothing left. No tears, no anger, no sadness. She sat on the cold steps and stared out at nothing. She was numb. She sat like that for another hour until her mother staggered up the sidewalk. "Hi, Hun!"

Cathy, Kenny and Susan

CHAPTER TWENTY-SIX

Stratford-Spring 1960

If Cathy hoped things would get better, she was wrong. She really started to wonder what was wrong with Mrs. Wrenn. She started to wonder why she and her husband adopted Kenny and Susan. Mrs. Wrenn treated Cathy horribly, but she didn't treat Kenny and Susan very well either. She fed them, made sure they went to bed, and washed their clothes, but she never touched them. She never showed them any affection. She didn't really act like their mother. She seemed more like a caretaker of some sort.

Did she adopt them because she was motherly and wanted to have children that she could love and that would love her? Cathy didn't think so. Cathy knew that the government sent the Wrenns a cheque every month and she thought the money was supposed to help out with the children. That's why Cathy thought Mrs. Wrenn rented out the apartment to her mother, so that she could have extra money coming in, and also why she charged Rita to take care of Cathy, although she did the exact opposite of taking care. Was she in it just for the money? Did she resent having to take care of Kenny and Susan? She certainly resented having Cathy and Rita around. Cathy guessed she would never know. But one thing she knew for sure was that it was getting harder and harder to live at Mrs. Wrenn's.

One reason was because her mom was gone so much. Another was that Kenny and Susan seemed to be growing more and more distant from their "parents" and they were getting quieter and more depressed. If there was any bright side for Cathy, it was that she at least had a real mother. Poor Kenny and Susan were adopted, and Cathy wondered if they wished their real parents would have kept them. Cathy started to feel sorry for them because she knew that as soon as she was old enough she would go back to Cape Breton, but those kids had nowhere to go. Maybe she would try to be a little nicer to them from now on.

Her mother was also not getting any better. She worked hard at the Laundry, but she continued to come home late every night and be gone out most of the weekend. They hadn't been to visit Doug and Elsie for ages, and it seemed like Uncle Stan and Aunt Joanie were busy with their own kids. They hadn't been to visit Uncle Frank and Aunt Kay in months; for some reason her mom decided she didn't want to go back to Brantford any time soon.

She also said they couldn't afford to go back down home again this summer because they were just there last summer when Papa died. The idea of spending another long summer with Mrs. Wrenn made Cathy want to be sick to her stomach.

Cathy's routine hadn't changed much. She would wake up in the morning at the same time as her mom, and then as soon as she went to work, Cathy would go back to bed for an hour or so. Mrs. Wrenn would come up and check the room to make sure Cathy was "behaving" and then huff back down the stairs. After all these years, she would still remind Cathy that she wasn't allowed to touch Kenny's bed. Cathy wondered when the heck Kenny would finally be old enough to have his sacred bed.

She would have her tea and toast, go to school, then come back again at the end of the day with a feeling of dread to see what Mrs. Wrenn had in store for her. Sometimes the door was locked and she would hang around the yard until Mrs. Wrenn let her in. Other times, she would be able to get in the house but Mrs. Wrenn would send her back out again.

Most of the time though, she was allowed in and she would play with Kenny and Susan in the living room and then they would all eat supper together in the kitchen. No one spoke during the meal; Mrs. Wrenn just scowled at everyone; Mr. Wrenn avoided any eye contact by reading the Beacon; and the kids would stare at their plates and eat their tasteless food. They were all relieved when the meal was finally over so they could disappear to different corners of the house. Mrs. Wrenn stayed in the kitchen for hours after Mr. Wrenn went to his room and the kids went to the living room.

Once Cathy was finished cleaning up, which she did as fast as possible because nothing made her skin crawl more than being alone with Mrs. Wrenn in the kitchen, she would meet up with Kenny and Susan in front of the TV. After a while, Mrs. Wrenn would send Cathy upstairs and she would wait for her mom, who never came, and then she'd get ready and go to bed. So went the days.

One particular evening, Cathy was very tired and feeling extra depressed about her life. Knowing that she wasn't going to Cape Breton this summer cast a shadow over her that kept her in a dark mood most of the time. Instead of heading into the living room after supper, Kenny and Susan were up in Kenny's room playing Cowboys and Indians. Cathy was curious about the change of scenery, so she went up after them and sat on the floor to watch them play.

"Pow pow pow! You're dead, Injuns!" Kenny cried as he knocked down all of Susan's Indians.

"Oh no we're not! You're dead!" Susan jumped up and shot Kenny with her pretend bow and arrow.

"I'm an Indian too!" Cathy joined in and she danced a circle around Kenny. Susan danced around with Cathy and soon they were shooting and dancing and falling down as they got shot.

They must have crashed to the floor too loudly because they stopped when they heard Mrs. Wrenn clomping heavily up the stairs.

"What the hell is going on up here?" she screeched at them. The kids froze and stared at Mrs. Wrenn.

"I asked you a bloody question. What the hell is going on here, you're about to fall through the ceiling!"

"Nothing, Mom—we're just playing Cowboys and Indians," answered Kenny. He looked nervous; Mrs. Wrenn was more angry than usual.

"Yes, Mommy, we're having fun. Look at all the dead Indians." Poor little Susan was trying to divert her mother's attention.

"And what are you doing up here, Cathy? You know I don't like you to be in the children's rooms!"

"I'm sorry. I thought it would be OK for me to play up here," Cathy said quietly.

"Children, get downstairs in that living room. Cathy, you clean this mess up, all of it!" She said through clenched teeth. Kenny and Susan glanced quickly at Cathy, but they didn't say a word and they didn't try to help.

"Can't Kenny and Susan stay to help me?" she asked.

"If I wanted them to help you, I would have told them to help you."

"Well that's just not fair! We were all playing. This isn't even my room!" Cathy's voice rose in anger. She felt all of the blood drain out of her face and she started shaking. She looked at the kids, silently pleading with them to stick up for her. They both looked away and headed for the door. They were just leaving her there so they could go watch their stupid TV!

"No! Wait! You two have to help me. I'm not doing this alone!" Cathy yelled at their backs. But they didn't turn around, they just ignored her. Mrs. Wrenn's eyes were bulging out of her head.

"You shut your mouth, young Miss and do what I tell you!" Mrs. Wrenn came across the room and Cathy thought she was going to hit her. At first, Cathy saw red, and then all she saw was black.

"Get the hell away from me you WITCH!" She took a step towards Mrs. Wrenn and pushed her backwards. Mrs. Wrenn looked like she was going to lose her mind. Cathy took another step towards her, pushed her again and screamed, "I hate you! I HATE you! You're a fucking WITCH, and I wish you would DIE!"

All of a sudden Mr. Wrenn was in the room and with both hands he grabbed Cathy by her shoulders and shook her. Cathy fell to the floor and he stumbled to catch her. He wrapped his arms around her and didn't let go until all the energy ran out of her body. She was sobbing and saying, "I hate her." Over and over again.

"Go call her mother," Mr. Wrenn ordered his wife. His voice was low but it was stern. Mrs. Wrenn didn't say a word. She just turned and left the room.

Cathy wasn't sure how much later her mother arrived home, and she couldn't really recall what had happened after Mr. Wrenn walked into Kenny's room. She just knew she was in her own bed, under the blankets, and her mother was sitting beside her and holding a cold cloth on her forehead.

"Are you OK, Cathy?" Her mother asked quietly. "You gave Mr. and Mrs. Wrenn quite a scare. They said you were acting like you had the devil in you. What happened?"

She was about to tell her mother how Mrs. Wrenn was going to make her clean up the room while the kids went downstairs, but she realized there was no point. Her mother would just tell her she had over-reacted, that she was just tired, or that she should have done what she was told.

"Mommy, I hate her. I hate Mrs. Wrenn and I want to leave," was all she could manage to say. Then her mother surprised her.

"Well, Hun, I've been thinking. Mama's birthday is coming up in April and even though I can't really afford it, I'm going to buy two train tickets for us to go down home. Would you like that?" Her mother smiled at her and touched her cheek.

Cathy closed her eyes when the tears started streaming down her cheeks. As much as she wanted to be furious with her mother for not sticking up for her against Mrs. Wrenn, she felt so completely exhausted that just the thought of going home to Cape Breton, made her feel more calm.

"Yes." She opened her eyes again. "Please, take me home."

Little Johnny, Georgie, Janey, Marlene and Nana

CHAPTER TWENTY-SEVEN

Cape Breton-Spring 1960

A few weeks later, Cathy's whole family was at Nana's house celebrating her birthday.

"Happy birthday, dear Mama! Happy birthday, to you!" They all clapped and laughed and kissed Nana on the cheek. Nana smiled at her children and grandchildren as she started to cut her cake. She was 57 years old today, and although Cathy knew her grandmother felt 20 years older than that, she looked happy that her family was gathered around her. She seemed extra happy that Rita and Cathy came home unexpectedly; it had only been a year since Papa died and Cathy knew Nana was still having a hard time.

"Happy birthday, Mama!" Rita said as she took the knife from her mother to finish cutting the cake for everyone.

Big Molly was there with her growing brood, Aunt Alice came up with Little Johnny and Georgie, and of course Marlene and Janey were there too. Francis was also there, and Cathy secretly hoped he'd leave soon. He was dating a girl named Wilma and Nana didn't like her, so she wasn't allowed at the party. Francis was ranting and raving about not having his girlfriend there, but eventually he gave up and went downtown.

"Here, Rita, give that to me. We'll all be right starvin' by the time you get around to cutting the cake." Cathy's Aunt Alice took the knife and quickly sliced her way into the cake.

"Oh, thanks, dear—my hand was getting sore anyway." Rita smiled at her younger sister and went and sat down on the couch. Cathy saw her Aunt Alice roll her eyes before she shot a look at Big Molly.

"C'mon now kids, gather round, gather round. This cake won't eat itself." Aunt Alice motioned for everyone to get in the cake line.

"Me first, me first!" Janey squealed as she butted in front of Marlene.

"Oh for God's sake, you're all going to get some, so quit your screeching," Aunt Alice laughed as she gave Janey a huge piece.

"Here you go Mama, a nice slice just for you." Aunt Alice handed a plate to her mother.

"Not right now Alice, I want to sit and talk with your sister. Now, Rita dear, tell me all about what you've been up to in Ontario."

Alice pursed her lips together and shoved the plate at Marlene. She went over to stand beside Big Molly, crossed her arms, and mumbling out of the side of her mouth.

"Well, I just went from being in a good mood to a bad mood in two minutes! It's always the same when Rita comes home. Everyone is always all 'ga-ga goo-goo' over her and I haven't the faintest idea why." Alice looked sharply out of the corner of her eye toward Molly, but Molly just stared down at her cake.

"I mean, really! Rita left home years ago to make a life for herself up in Ontario," Alice continued. "But what did she do? She did a bit of work in the factory and then spent the rest of her time chasing men, drinking, smoking, and carrying on. Then she goes and gets pregnant, takes care of the baby for a couple years, then gets sick of her and gives the poor thing up. What was she thinking, Molly? Didn't she know that Mama was done taking care of babies? In my opinion, Rita should have just come home, got a little place of her own and looked after that sweet little angel by herself."

Without so much as a word, Molly scraped the rest of her cake into the garbage pail and put her plate in the sink. Alice, still talking, cornered her at the counter.

"Little pitchers have big ears, Alice," Molly said as she motioned toward where Cathy was sitting at the kitchen table.

"But God Almighty," Alice huffed, as if she didn't catch on. "She left her baby here and went back to Ontario. To do what,

I ask you? More men and more drinking? Lord knows she couldn't get herself married. Then she has the nerve to take little Cathy back to Ontario with her! The poor little dear, being taken away from the only home she ever knew to go live with a perfect stranger."

Molly looked at her with surprise and raised her eyebrows, "Alice!"

"Well, she may have met Rita a few times, Molly, but little Cathy sure didn't have a relationship with her."

"Then when poor Daddy dies," she went on again, "and she flies in like she owns the place, going on about how much she loved him. Loved him? 'You left him!' I'd like to tell her. 'You broke Daddy's heart when you left and then you broke it again when you took Cathy away from him.' The only thing that made him happy after Rita left, as far as I'm concerned, was me."

Cathy often overheard her Aunt Alice tell anyone who would listen about how she always felt proud of herself for doing the right thing. She got married early to a good man, had her son, Little Johnny, and then her daughter, Georgie, and finally her dark-haired boy, Frank. She had a cute house that was always kept spic and span. She took care of her family and made sure they were always neat and tidy, and she went to church every Sunday. "You couldn't say that about Rita," Alice was known to say. "Everyone thinks she has the world by the tail. Why? Just because she's pretty? Because she can sing and tell a joke? Well, you need a lot more than a pretty face to make it in this world. You need to have God in your life, you need to work hard, and you need to take care of your children. And as far as I'm concerned, Rita has not taken good care of that child."

Cathy continued to eat Nana's birthday cake and tried to pretend she couldn't overhear her aunts talking. While her Aunt Alice was doing all the talking; poor Aunt Molly looked like she wanted the floor to swallow her up. As much as it made Cathy feel embarrassed for her mother, she wanted to keep listening because she was curious about all the things her aunt had to say.

"And you can tell when you look into that little girl's eyes," Cathy heard Aunt Alice whisper, "she's not happy. She's depressed. It doesn't take a scientist to see that our little niece is being mistreated. Just look at Rita over there, telling jokes like nothing's going on. My God, Molly, it's taking every ounce of my strength not to go over there and smack that smile off Rita's face and knock some sense into her."

But of course, Cathy knew that Aunt Alice would do no such thing, she wouldn't say a word. Aunt Alice knew that her mother and Nana had a relationship that no one could penetrate. Nana always said that the sun rose and set on her eldest daughter, and nothing Alice had to say would change that.

After everyone finished their cake and tea, Aunt Alice gathered up her kids, and with a quick goodbye left the house. Cathy didn't think she'd plan on coming again while Rita was there.

Everyone had cleared out of the house, Rita had finished up the dishes, and Molly had sent her kids back home with Rolfe.

When it was time for bed, Rita and Molly hugged and kissed Cathy, Marlene, and Janey, and tucked them under the covers. Rita noticed that Molly gave Janey an extra-long hug before she turned out the light and shut the bedroom door. The sisters went into the living room to join their mother.

Finally, Rita had a minute to talk to her mother without all the noise and chaos of their large family.

"Oh, Mama, life isn't easy up in Ontario," Rita told her mother. "It's not going a'tall the way I wanted it to."

"Well, what's Walter saying? Is he planning on marrying you soon?" her mother asked quietly while she rocked in her chair.

"You've been dating him for ages, haven't you Rita?" Molly asked as she sat down on the couch next to her sister.

"Oh dear God, Molly, it's been more than five years, but he won't marry me because he doesn't want to take care of Cathy," Rita whispered knowing the girls had just gone to bed.

"G'wan, Rita! Won't take care of her?" her mother whispered back. "He should be happy to have a daughter like Cathy, she's the sweetest girl in the world."

"I know Mama, but he wants Reg to pay for her. And unless I can get him to, Walter won't marry me."

"Well, there you have your answer then Rita, you'll have to break up with him. I mean what kind of a man wouldn't help take care of an innocent little girl?" asked Molly.

Both Mama and Rita quickly looked away and a tense silence filled the air. Molly widened her eyes at their reaction and jumped off the couch. "Well, I guess I should head back home. Rolfe will be wondering where I got to." She quickly gathered her things and headed out the door.

Rita and her mother sat quietly for a few minutes.

Her mother continued to rock in her chair, then she looked at Rita with her big brown eyes.

"What is it, Mama? What are you thinking?"

"Cathy doesn't look too good, Rita," she said quietly.

"What do you mean? She looks fine; she's pretty as a picture!"

"She's pretty, my dear, but the light has gone out of her eyes and I'm worried about her."

"Well I must say she got real upset at Mrs. Wrenn just before we came here, and I don't think she's gotten over it."

"What are you going to do about it, Rita? You can't keep living with that woman. My God there's got to be another apartment you can live in, surely?" She raised her eyebrows as she rocked.

"I'll figure something out. Anyway, how about you, Mama? How are you doing?" Rita changed the subject.

Mama sighed and looked out the window. "Well your father's gone, God bless his soul."

Rita changed the subject again. "How's Francis? Who's this girlfriend he's got?"

Mama looked back at Rita. "Her name's Wilma. I had her coming in once a week to help with the house because my side has been painin' and it's hard to get all the work done. She's a good worker and I thought she was a nice girl, but one morning I woke up and found her and Francis sleeping on the couch! I don't know what they were up to, but I told her to get out of the house. Francis was mad as all get out and he told me that he loved her and wanted her to move in here. I told him, over my dead body!"

"So what's he going to do now? Will he finally move out?"

"Well, I can't really have him move out dear, he's the only one bringing any money home. That cheque I get from your poor father wouldn't even feed the chickens." Mama sighed again.

"Besides, Francis thinks this house is his, and he's not leaving it. He told me last week that he wants Wilma to move in and sleep upstairs with him in the room."

"Just tell him no, Mama. This is still your house," Rita said impatiently.

"You think he'll listen to me, Rita? You've got another thing coming…he thinks I should move out!"

"Well that's not going to happen. I wish Dougie was here, he'd talk sense to him."

"Anyway dear, I don't want to talk about it anymore. It just upsets me. Let's get up to bed."

They got ready for bed and got under the covers. Rita snuggled up to her mother and they both lay there together and said their prayers. Rita remembered when she was a little girl and her mother would tell her to repeat after her. "Our Father, who art in heaven…" And just as Rita would repeat after her, her mother would go onto the next line and then the next and the next; little Rita couldn't catch up. Rita laughed at the memory.

"C'mon now, say your prayers Rita, and quit your carrying on." Rita could almost see Mama smiling in the dark.

Janey, Marlene, Cathy and Bimbo

CHAPTER TWENTY-EIGHT

Cape Breton-Summer 1960

Cathy didn't have to beg this time. Rita gave no argument when Mama told her that Cathy was staying for the summer. Rita didn't have the energy to insist that her daughter go back to Ontario with her. She realized deep down that it would be a lot easier for her to simply go to work, go out with Walter, and spend as little time as possible at 28 Brant Street. Without having to worry about Cathy getting into trouble with Mrs. Wrenn, and without the constant threat that she and Cathy would get kicked out, the summer would be quiet and Rita could concentrate on getting that ring on her finger. Maybe if she was able to make Walter realize that Cathy didn't cost much to raise; just a little bit of food and some clothing was all she needed, then maybe he would re-think his decision about having Reg support Cathy and not him.

"It's a good decision you made, dear. Leaving Cathy with me this summer will do her good," Mama said as she hugged Rita goodbye once again at the train station.

"Yes, Mama, I agree with you," said Rita. "I just hope that by the end of the summer, when I come back to get her, I'll show her my engagement ring and I'll be able to announce that we're moving in with Walter. If I can just have some help from Walter, to make sure we have a little place to live in and enough money to pay our bills, I'm sure we'll all be happier."

Rita crossed her fingers hoping against all hope that her life would take a turn for the better in a few months. She deserved to be happy, didn't she? Hadn't she worked long enough and hard enough? Didn't she deserve a break? No one knew how hard it was to raise a child on their own. There were so many feelings of guilt and a sense that you were always doing something wrong. She always made sure that Cathy was well-fed and well-dressed, clean, and healthy. Why didn't anyone give her any credit for how hard it was for her? She didn't think anyone had a clue what it was like to be a single mother.

She bet that most women in her place would have given up their baby. But she didn't. She kept her baby, and she was confused as to why she never got a pat on the back for it. There were only a few short years when Cathy had to live with Mama and Daddy, but they understood that it was only while she got back on her feet again. And as soon as she could, she took her daughter back and did her very best to take care of her.

She wondered if Cathy even appreciated what she had sacrificed to keep her. If she hadn't gotten pregnant, she would be married to Reg Larion or Walter by now. Of course, she wouldn't give Cathy up for the world now. She loved her daughter more than anything. It was just that sometimes she would like some acknowledgment for her hard work and maybe some love in return.

Cathy hadn't told her she loved her since she could remember, and lately whenever she tried to hug or kiss her, Cathy got stiff and acted is if she couldn't wait to get away from her. It hurt her feelings so much when Cathy would be cold to her. She never hit Cathy or said mean things to her. She didn't know why Cathy acted this way. Cathy didn't even seem to care that she wouldn't see her for the next four months. When they said their goodbyes, Cathy just gave her an awkward kiss on the cheek and ran out of the house.

"Oh, Cathy! I'm so happy that you're staying here with us!" Marlene smiled from ear to ear when Cathy told her and Janey that Nana put her foot down and insisted that she stay for the rest of the school year and the whole summer. The three girls had already eaten their lunch and had the rest of the afternoon to do whatever they wanted. They could play hide-and-go-seek, tag, or red light/green light. For now, they were sitting in the long grass in the yard watching the crazy dog running around like a maniac. The summer heat felt good on their backs and the cool breeze off the ocean was comforting. Cathy loved the breeze when it blew her hair back from her face and kept those little stray hairs from tickling her nose.

Earlier in the day, Nana had taken the girls to visit Papa's grave over on Wallace's Road. She said she wasn't feeling good when they got back, so she went in the house to lie down. The girls had never seen Nana lie down in the afternoon before, so they thought they better head outside and let her be—plus Francis wasn't home from work yet, and for once the house was empty and quiet so Nana could finally rest.

Janey was playing with a long piece of grass and being quieter than usual. Normally, the tiny little thing was a going concern. She liked to make sure she knew what was going on at all times; she hated when anyone kept secrets from her. She always listened when the adults talked, and if it wasn't for her, Cathy and Marlene would never know what was going on.

Cathy knew that Janey had always been really close to Nana and she hated to have Nana out of her sight. That's why she didn't go to school much. She often let on to Nana that she was sick or something so that Nana would let her stay home. But she wasn't sick, she just wanted to be home and make sure Nana was OK. She stuck to her side like glue most of the time. Cathy didn't really understand why Janey was like that. She thought Nana was perfectly capable of taking care of herself, and besides, what was Janey going to do to help her? She was so small and skinny, she could hardly lift a twig.

Cathy realized that even Marlene seemed quieter than usual. She didn't often say much. She mostly just looked at you with her eyebrows raised as if to say, "See? See what I mean?" Cathy always nodded like she knew what she meant, but more often than not, she had no idea what Marlene was thinking about.

Suddenly, both Marlene and Janey looked down the road. They jumped up and started running in the opposite direction. Cathy had no idea what was going on. She tried to see what they had been looking at, and then she saw Francis coming home from work. He was stumbling and swaying as he was making his way towards the house. It was only late afternoon; he shouldn't even be home yet.

"Cathy! C'mon!" hissed Janey from behind the shed. She gestured wildly for Cathy to run.

"What's the matter with you two?" Cathy huffed as she got in behind the shed. The two girls were sitting on the ground with their backs to the shed wall, and Marlene had her finger on her lips.

"You have to be quiet, Cathy, or he'll hear us," Janey whispered.

"Who? Francis?"

"Yes, Francis. Of course, Francis. Who else?" Janey rolled her eyes. "Don't you know how crazy he is?"

"Crazy? I always thought he was kind of grumpy, but I didn't think he was crazy."

"Well ever since Papa died, he's not been right," said Marlene.

"Tell her what he did that one night, Mar," said Janey.

"He was after drinking all day downtown when we saw him coming up the tracks," Marlene began. "He was swaying and stumbling, kicking rocks and swearing and muttering. I guess he was mad as a hatter because he didn't get paid for all the coal he brought up. He must have taken whatever money he had left over and drank it all at the tavern. We were all in the kitchen cleaning the dishes when he came in." Marlene opened her eyes wide and raised her eyebrows. Cathy shook her head, not understanding.

"What? What happened?"

"He went to light the stove because he was hungry and Ma didn't have any food on for him," she continued. "He was making all kinds of noise and stumbling around the room and when he saw there was no wood in the bin, he got right angry. He swore at Ma, right to her face. We couldn't believe it. He'd never done that before. But ever since Papa died, he's been right nuts." Marlene looked at Janey. Janey was rapidly nodding her head up and down in agreement.

"He kicked the door on his way out and almost took the thing off its hinges. We all hoped he'd gone back downtown to stay with Wilma instead of here, but we heard him outside swearing and going on."

Janey joined in. "We watched out the window as he got the axe from the shed and started chopping wood. He could hardly hit the wood and he kept missing and swinging and then missing again. He was getting some mad then. He grabbed a few pieces of wood and came in the house. He threw the wood in the bin and he was swearing and kicking and still holding the axe." She looked back at Marlene.

"He turned to us and started yelling at Ma about where was his food and why didn't she cook him something and why should he have to light the fire, it should be ready to go by the time he got home," Marlene continued.

"Ma kept trying to say she was sorry but she was scared to death. We all backed up over by the window and he kept coming, yelling and holding that axe. Janey was crying and Ma was trying to hide her behind her dress. It's like Francis was blind or something because he didn't see me when I got around behind him and over to the sink. The cast iron pan was there on the stove. I took it, got up behind him, and hit him as hard as I could! I couldn't reach his head, but I got him a good one in the arm," Marlene said proudly.

"Lord, did he ever howl then!" Janey went on. "He dropped the axe and turned around and he was screaming and spitting and I thought Marlene was done for."

"Get out! Get out of here Francis or God will punish you!" Marlene had jumped up and was acting the whole thing out.

Cathy couldn't get over it. What the hell was wrong with Francis? Was he insane?

"Yep, that's how it went. Then he told us all to go to hell and he ran right out of the house," said Janey. "We didn't see him again that night, thank God."

"So that's why we're hiding? He's drunk now like he was before?" Cathy worried.

Marlene raised her eyebrows and said, "Let's go down to Mrs. MacIntyre's place. We can stay there until Francis leaves again."

"But what about Ma? We can't just leave her there!" cried Janey.

"She'll have locked herself in the room by now. He won't get her," Marlene answered. Janey looked doubtful, but Marlene had already started walking down the road. Cathy and Janey reluctantly followed her; Marlene always knew what to do when Francis was acting crazy, so it was best to go with her.

Cathy thought there was nothing worse than Mrs. Wrenn and the way she treated her, but Francis was their uncle; she couldn't believe that he was carrying on like this. But just seeing how afraid Marlene and Janey were of him scared Cathy too. It was a good thing she was going to be here this summer, so she could save everyone from Francis.

The three girls stuck together like glue for the rest of the summer. They made sure that they helped Nana with all the housework, always kept food ready for when Francis got home, and kept the wood bin full and the stove lit. They all slept in the room together with the door locked, and whenever Francis came up the road, swaying and stumbling, they would run out the back door and head to Mrs. MacIntyre's until the coast was clear.

The Avon River in Stratford

CHAPTER TWENTY-NINE

Stratford-Fall 1960

Life was like a roller coaster. One minute she was in Cape Breton with Nana, Marlene and Janey, and the next minute she wasn't. In Cape Breton she was with her family, friends, and neighbours, with the freedom to run, play, and laugh, knowing that no matter where you went, you were always welcome. You didn't have to knock on doors or ask permission to come inside. If the girls went to Aunt Tussie's, they were welcomed in and given cookies or buns or whatever Aunt Tussie could find in her cupboard. If they took the bus up to Mitchell Avenue, Big Molly always had her arms open and took them all in, gave them tea and something to eat, and then sent them into the backyard to play with their cousins.

Even Aunt Alice, who liked to have more order in her life, hugged and kissed them when they arrived on her door step and herded them in and arranged them all around her kitchen table. She would ask them what they wanted, give them two or three options, then when the girls would pick one thing, she would end up putting all three things on their plates anyway. Laughing, she would offer them more and more until their stomachs burst. She would have them giggling on the floor when she'd tell them her stories. She'd stand up and make sweeping hand gestures and use different voices for different characters and personalities. Aunt Alice was the funniest one of the bunch; she reminded Cathy a lot of Aunt Kay.

No matter where the girls would find themselves—at the store, at the park, down on the beach or walking through the fields—they knew everyone they met and everyone knew they were the Barron girls. They were like the Three Musketeers.

But just as life went up, and was happy and carefree, life would go back down, and Cathy would find herself, once again, in the stuffy dark attic room at 28 Brant Street with her mother. When Rita came from Ontario to get her, there was no ring, no marriage, and no plan for moving out of Mrs. Wrenn's.

School was starting in early September and even though Cathy had every intention of staying in Cape Breton for the school year, she found herself on the train heading back to

Ontario to start grade five at St. Joseph's Catholic School in Stratford, and not at St. John's with Marlene and Janey, like she had hoped.

"Well, Cathy-o, I can't tell you how happy I am that you're back with me," her mother said as she put the laundry away. "It was a sad and lonely summer without you, Hun."

Cathy didn't think her mother looked good. She seemed tired and pale; her hair was frizzy and needed a cut. She was smoking one cigarette after another and Cathy noticed there were more wrinkles around her eyes and mouth than before. She wasn't talking as much as usual and she often stared into space, far away in her thoughts. Cathy was worried about her. She had hoped against hope that Walter would have proposed to her mother while she was away in Cape Breton.

If he wasn't going to propose, why did he bother dating her and taking her out all the time? Why didn't her mother just give up on him? There must be other men out there, ones that wouldn't mind a 10-year-old girl tagging along.

"Don't worry, Mom. I'm here with you now. Everything will be OK," she said as she went to her mother and patted her on the shoulder. She couldn't bring herself to hug her. It had been months since they'd seen each other, and even though Cathy knew she loved her mother, something kept her from wanting to comfort her.

"Thanks, Hun," Rita touched her daughter's hand. "I'm going out tonight with Walter, so I might be a little late getting home, OK?"

That's a real surprise Cathy thought, taking her hand away from her mother's shoulder. What was the point of her coming back here to live with her mom, if all she ever did was go out? She was filled with familiar feelings of frustration and loneliness. She shook her head. Why couldn't she just stay in Cape Breton?

Just as her mother said, she was late getting home. Cathy had played outside for as long as she could before it got dark and Mrs. Wrenn made her come in. She ate supper with Kenny and Susan. The food was bland and there was so much tension in the air that as soon as Cathy cleaned up the dishes, she headed up to her room to get away from the heaviness of it all. She got ready for bed and read her book under the covers for as long as she could.

Her eyes had grown heavy and as soon as she put the book down, she had fallen asleep.

She wasn't sure how long she'd been sleeping when she was woken up by the sound of whispering. She held her breath and listened. She heard her mom giggle and then cough. Cathy could smell cigarette smoke and something else. Cologne? Then she heard a man's voice.

"Shhhh Rita, she'll hear you." It was Walter.

"Don't worry, she's sound asleep. I come in every night and she never wakes up," whispered her mother.

Cathy couldn't believe that her mother had Walter up here. He wasn't allowed in the house, let alone up in the room. She could hear creaking and just as she realized they were on Kenny's bed, she heard Mrs. Wrenn.

"Rita! You better not be on Kenny's bed!" Mrs. Wrenn's voice drifted from the bottom of the stairs.

Cathy saw her mother and Walter freeze. My God, how could that woman know that someone was on the bed?

Her mother jumped up and ran to the stairs. "Oh, sorry, Mrs. Wrenn," she whispered into the stairwell. "I'll get off right now. Good night."

"That was a close one," she giggled to Walter.

"Do you think she heard me?" he asked.

"God, no. If she heard you, do you think we'd still be standing here right now?" She put her arms around him and they started kissing.

Cathy was shocked. They were kissing right here, in the room, where she was sleeping. She closed her eyes and hoped that they were kissing goodbye and that he was leaving soon. She hated the sound of their kissing; it made her skin crawl.

Suddenly, there was a weight on the bed by her feet. She opened her eyes and in the gloom, she could tell that they were both lying on the bed. She stopped breathing. Did they really think she was asleep? All she could smell now was cologne, cigarettes and beer.

Her mother stopped giggling and Walter was breathing hard. Suddenly she heard her mother make a small gasp and Walter grunted.

What were they doing??

They stopped moving and then there was silence in the room.

Cathy wanted to vomit. She felt sick to her stomach. She just realized what they were doing, what they had done.

The weight lifted off her legs and she pulled them up so she was in a little ball. She moved as close to the wall as she could and kept her eyes shut. She didn't make a sound. She could hear Walter mumbling goodbye to her mother and slowly creeping down the stairs. She heard her mother light a cigarette, and the smell of the smoke made Cathy want to be sick. Her mind was racing. How could her mother have done that? Did she really think that she couldn't hear them? Was she so desperate to marry Walter that she would do that with him, while her daughter was in the very same bed?? They were disgusting. They made her sick. They were gross pigs!

The next day after Cathy got back from school, she was surprised to see her mother sitting on the front steps. She was pale as a ghost and was shaking like a leaf. Cathy was still so upset with her that she couldn't bring herself to care about what was wrong with her mother. She stepped around her and started to go in the house.

"Cathy."

She stopped. Her mother's voice sounded flat and lifeless.

"She kicked us out."

Cathy blinked. "What? She kicked us out? Mrs. Wrenn?"

"She was waiting for me this morning and before I left the house she told me that we had to leave."

"Why?" Cathy asked, but she knew why.

"She said that I broke the rules. She said it was because I sat on Kenny's bed."

Mrs. Wrenn was horrible and she was mean, but she wasn't stupid. There's no way that her mother could have snuck Walter in and out of the house without Mrs. Wrenn knowing. She knew every sound and creak in that house, and Cathy was sure it wasn't the creak of Kenny's bed that put Mrs. Wrenn over the edge.

Cathy didn't know how to feel. She wanted to feel happy that they were leaving Mrs. Wrenn's, but she was still so disgusted with her mother that she couldn't bring herself to feel anything.

"When?"

"We have to be gone by this weekend. She's only giving me four days to find another place."

"Well, what did you think, Mom? Did you think she didn't hear you and Walter last night? Do you think that I didn't hear you or feel you on my legs?" Cathy came back down the steps and stood in front of her mother. "What is the matter with you?" she shouted. "Did you really think I was sleeping for God's sake?"

"Cathy we weren't doing anything! Walter was just kissing me. I'm sorry!" Rita started crying.

"Oh, stop your crying Mom. Stop being such an actress! I know what you two were doing and I think you're sick!"

She nearly stepped on her mother's foot as she rushed past her and into the house. She slammed the door and ran up the stairs.

Rita and Cathy

CHAPTER THIRTY

Stratford-Fall 1960

It didn't take long for them to pack up their few belongings. They had the same two blue suitcases they'd arrived with and a few cardboard boxes to hold their dishes, books, pictures, and other things they had collected over the years. Her mother said that Walter was going to come and help them move, but he got called into work and wasn't going to show up.

Cathy was only just starting to speak to her mother. The shock over her and Walter carrying on in the bed was starting to subside. She was still disgusted, but her mother wouldn't admit to what she'd done. She'd just kept acting innocent and pretending they were only kissing. Cathy wanted to believe that was true, if for no other reason than to be able to get over it and be happy about the move.

It really sunk in that they were finally moving out of the Wrenn's the day after her mother told her. When she got home from school, Kenny and Susan ran down the stairs to meet her on the sidewalk.

"Is it true Cathy? Are you really moving?" Susan asked with tears in her eyes.

"Of course it's true, dummy. Mom told us this morning. They're moving out on the weekend. Right, Cathy?" Kenny said as he elbowed his sister in her side.

"Ow! Stop that, Kenny!" Susan said as she elbowed him back. "I don't want you to leave, Cathy! I'm going to miss you."

She started crying and Cathy felt bad. Susan was a nice little girl and the poor thing had to have Mrs. Wrenn as a mother.

She hugged Susan. "It's OK. I'll come back and play with you sometimes. You'll still see me." She looked over Susan's head at Kenny and saw that he had tears in his eyes too. Cathy felt a surge of emotion. She had lived with these two for more than five years, and even though they didn't always get along, she had grown used to them. She wiped away her own tears.

"Come on! Let's go play kick the can." Kenny ran to find an old can in the shed.

"Do you promise, Cathy? Do you promise you'll come and visit me?" Susan looked at her with desperation.

"I promise." And after giving her another hug, they ran and chased after Kenny and his can.

"OK, I think that's about it then," her mother said as she did the final sweep of the room. "Uncle Stan will be here in a few minutes to take us to our new place, Cathy-o, so come on down when you're ready." She picked up her suitcase and went downstairs to pay Mrs. Wrenn the final rent.

Her mom had found a place pretty quickly. Uncle Stan had put an ad on the board at Fischer's that they were looking for a cheap apartment somewhere uptown. Within a day, Uncle Stan got the number of the landlord who rented apartments on Wellington Street.

They were to move into 50 Wellington Street that Sunday. Cathy shook her head and closed her eyes praying for patience when she heard that. Within a few days? It was that easy to get an apartment? Why on earth didn't her mother do this years ago?

Regardless, once she realized that they were really leaving this horrible place where they'd lived for so many years, a sense of peace came over her like a warm blanket. She always thought she'd be jumping for joy and laughing and shouting from the roof tops when they finally left, but she found instead that her joy was calm, quiet, and still.

Along with the sense of peace, a tiny little flicker of hope had started to grow. Would this be a new beginning? Would her mother stop drinking so much and come home after work? Would they eat supper together and go to bed at the same time?

Would there be a couch where they could curl up and read their books without feeling like someone was creeping up the stairs trying to catch them doing something wrong?

Cathy took a deep breath. She thanked God for allowing this to happen; for them getting kicked out and for finding an apartment so fast. Even though she would never forgive Walter and her mother for what they did on the bed, she thought maybe it was part of God's plan to get them out of Mrs. Wrenn's house. Lord knows her mother wouldn't have moved out on her own accord.

Cathy went to the empty dresser and looked in the mirror and gazed at the little girl's reflection. The girl looked older now; her cheeks were thinner, her eyes were darker, her baby teeth were gone, replaced by adult teeth. She had a more defined chin and jaw line and her hair was thicker and darker. She remembered the girl from five years ago—the one that left Cape Breton and came to Ontario. She had light in her eyes then. She had been happier, looked more innocent and more hopeful. She had been excited to start a new adventure with her mother. Her mother always talked so well of Ontario, and even though she didn't want to leave Nana, she was anxious to see it. Her mother told her that life in Ontario would be happy, that she would be loved and taken care of.

Life in Ontario was not happy. It was full of disappointments and shattered expectations. She wondered what life would have been like if her mother had let the nuns have her, if Reg would have married her, or if her mom would have kept her when she was a baby and not taken her to Cape

Breton in the first place. She wondered what life would have been like if her mother had left her in Cape Breton for good, and not taken her back to Ontario at all.

She knew her mother tried to take care of her and be a good mother, but she felt, so far, that her mother had failed.

Maybe once they got to Wellington Street, they could forget everything that happened at Mrs. Wrenn's house. Maybe they could start over. Maybe they would become closer and love each other more. Maybe Cathy would finally feel safe and secure.

Cathy peered into the mirror again and looked deep into the girl's eyes.

"It's all going to be OK now," she whispered. "We're finally getting away from Mrs. Wrenn and she'll never be able to bother us again."

She reached out and touched the girl's face. The girl always looked so sad, hurt, scared, and worried. Cathy thought if she could just take care of that little girl, hold her and rock her in her arms, maybe the girl would believe her when she told her everything was going to be alright. If somehow Cathy could make the girl believe that happiness was just around the corner, maybe on Wellington Street, then maybe Cathy would believe it too. She smiled, encouraging her friend to smile back.

And she did—a small smile, a worried smile, a doubtful smile.

With a sigh, Cathy moved away from the mirror, picked up her suitcase, and walked quietly down the stairs for the last time.

Cathy didn't see Mrs. Wrenn again until nine years later when she was up at the Stratford General having her first baby. Mrs. Wrenn was working in the hospital then and she came up to the nursery to give Cathy a greeting card.

Cathy was stunned. She couldn't believe that after all this time that woman would have the nerve to come into her room and deliver a greeting card.

Mrs. Wrenn had ruined her childhood; had caused her five years of loneliness and despair; had mentally abused her, and had made her feel stupid, ugly, and uncared for. Mrs. Wrenn had taken away her ability to love and trust her mother, and for many years to come Cathy suffered from the damage and the insecurities that Mrs. Wrenn created.

"I have to say that I hated that woman until the day she died…then I forgave her."

Taken from the diary of Catherine Barron
September 1989

A WOMAN'S STRENGTH…

For my mother, Catherine Barron, on her 60th birthday
April 18, 2010

As I sit here and look through all these pictures of Mom, Grandma, Nana, and myself—I feel overwhelmed. I realize there is a common thread that connects all us women together, but I'm not sure if I can put my finger on what it is. Is it simply that I'm part of the same line of mothers and daughters? Or is there something else? Something that speaks to me more than just the familiarity of our similar features.

After I visited with Mom today, I went back to the pile of photos. More recent images of Mom, so ravaged by cancer, remind me of Grandma's and Nana's pictures in their later years. I'm looking specifically at all three pairs of eyes and I see the similarity of their illnesses…their eyes are sunken and gaunt, tired and weary; all three women at their end had that same look.

But now I look more carefully at pictures of them when they were younger, when they were in their prime; wives to husbands; mothers to young children; friends to other women who liked to have a laugh, play cards, and share a cup of hot tea, and I see something else. Something I missed or maybe didn't realize before; it's their strength. All the strength in the world is calmly gazing at me from these smiling younger faces.

Nana's eyes show the strength it takes to deliver and care for ten babies with no money and poor living conditions. The strength to keep a house, send children to school in clean clothes, and have a warm stove for them to dress behind every morning. To take on the responsibility to raise three more girls; to make them feel like sisters; to give them a place to call home; a warm bed covered in coats. She not only had the strength of character to raise all these children, but to instill in them an enormous sense of spirituality that carried them through the ups and downs of their own lives.

Then I flip to a picture of Grandma: beautiful, stylish and courageous. The strength it would take to leave her family and start a new life, only to be faced with the biggest decision of all; in the spring of 1950, the decision to keep her baby, when everyone told her not to. She must have prayed every day for the right answer and God said, "Keep your baby girl."—and she did. To be single with a young child; to live away from her family and to work hard to make ends meet; to give that child shelter and food and a wonderful loving family of aunts and uncles that the little girl adored.

Maybe she knew she couldn't give her daughter everything, so she had the strength to send her away into the strong and loving arms of Nana, the one she knew could pick up where she left off; to succeed where she failed; to provide security and an environment that she knew she couldn't. And even though she made mistakes and caused some heartache, she succeeded in passing on this steely strength to her little girl, who grew up—needing it.

Now I search for the photo I so admire; her black hair, her porcelain skin, her shining eyes and of course that unmistakable strength that lies deep beneath their blue/gray colour. My mother certainly knew the strength she needed to get through the first seventeen years of her life, but did she have any idea how much more she would need?

Relationships that didn't turn out the way she wanted; loved ones that left her before she was ready; marriages that fell apart; and a sickness she couldn't fight. But through all those tough times, she tapped into the strength that she inherited from those women that came before her, and the strength she got from God and from her own strong spirit.

She, too, had children and had to work hard to make ends meet, to provide them with a clean house, nice clothes, to send them to camp, on trips, and to encourage them to play on teams and to dance; to be their own people, to be independent, be intelligent and to be good to others—to be successful in their lives through their careers and love lives. But most importantly, to be good parents, a good father and good mother to her beloved grandchildren.

Would this daughter of hers have the strength it takes to live a woman's life? Even with the loving environment she provided and raised her in? She knows life can be tough and unfair. Was she able to do it? Pass on this most important gift?

Then I turn over another photo and there I am, smiling and confident, and yes! There it is. That same strength. From Nana to Grandma to Mom and to me; I have the strength to be a good daughter, a good wife, and good friend—but most importantly, a good mother to my daughters.

Each life has been full of good times and bad, easy times and hard times, joys and sorrows, births and deaths. Each of us women have experienced the sheer and completely overwhelming happiness of being pregnant, having babies, nursing them and taking care of them and loving them like no other mother could.

Each mother, whether through her faith in God or faith in her own spirit, has passed on her gift of strength.

Did Mom know how much I would need? She probably hoped I wouldn't need as much as she and Grandma and Nana did. But here I am, sifting through these pictures, knowing my mother is dying. Needing to draw strength from somewhere, I realize all I need to do is look at these photos, look deep into their eyes, behind their laughter and their mischievous twinkles, and there it lies. The gift. The gift my mom gave me and the one I'm bound to give my daughters.

Will they need it? Please God, I hope not. But I will pass it on anyways, because they will be women one day, and they will need it.

Thank you, Mom, for everything. I couldn't have wished for a better mother. I love you and I will miss you every day of my life. Your little girl, Tara

My beautiful mother, Catherine, died on Sunday May 02, 2010.
She was 60 years old.

BIBLIOGRAPHY

Up the Humber to the West: My Métis Voyageurs
Joanne Doucette (© *Joanne Doucette, 2014 and 2016, revised 2016*)
https://liatris52.wordpress.com/up-the-humber-to-the-west-my-
metis-voyageurs/

Brantford History During the War
Gary Muir Copyright protected by Brantford Public Library
https://brantford.library.on.ca/archive/index.php/archive/article/160

BOOK CLUB QUESTIONS

1. Why didn't Cathy try harder to tell her family what was happening with Mrs. Wrenn?

2. What was going on in Rita's life that stopped her from being the kind of mother she should have been?

3. What does the reader think was "wrong" with Mrs. Wrenn?

4. Did the reader figure out who Janie's mother was?

5. If you were Rita, what would you have done differently?

6. Do you think Cathy would have been better off in Cape Breton? Why?

AUTHOR

Tara Mondou's life-long interest in reading books and telling stories has developed into a passion for writing and editing. As a first time author, she wrote, *Little Girl in the Mirror,* the heart-wrenching true story of her mother's childhood growing up in both Glace Bay, Nova Scotia and Stratford, Ontario in the 1950s.

Tara worked for Best Version Media as the Editor for *Neighbours of West Galt* and *Shade's Mills* magazines, two local publications in Cambridge, Ontario. Since 2009, she has been the chair person for the Waterloo Regional Block Parent® Program, developing programs that encourage children to be more physically active, healthy and safe.

In 2017, Tara co-founded a writers support group called Cambridge Authors, and continues to create opportunities and special events to help support and promote local writers and the literary arts.

Tara was the 2018 recipient of the Bernice Adams Memorial Award for Communication/Literary Arts, and volunteered as the Public Relations Director for Guitars for Kids Waterloo Region.

Tara lives in the West Galt area of Cambridge with her husband and their two daughters.

More information about Tara Mondou and her book *Little Girl in the Mirror* can be found at taramondou.com